"Who The Hell Are You?"

he demanded. Two tiny frown lines formed between his brows. His gaze was stony.

Her throat was suddenly clogged, and she had to swallow before she could speak. Connor O'Shaugnessy was easily the most intimidating person she had ever met. Fury radiated from him, and she stepped back. Advancing toward him wouldn't be wise, she knew, not unless he extended an invitation.

"Hi. I'm your postman." She flashed him her most engaging grin and earned a deeper scowl.

"I have a letter for you," she added, holding up her hand to show him. Connor O'Shaugnessy was definitely handsome, but at the moment he reminded her of a grizzly who could wipe her out with one swipe of his powerful hand.

Dear Reader:

Welcome! You hold in your hand a Silhouette Desire—your ticket to a whole new world of reading pleasure.

A Silhouette Desire is a sensuous, contemporary romance about passions, problems and the ultimate power of love. It is about today's woman—intelligent, successful, giving—but it is also the story of a romance between two people who are strong enough to follow their own individual paths, yet strong enough to compromise, as well.

These books are written by, for and about every woman that you are—wife, mother, sister, lover, daughter, career woman. A Silhouette Desire heroine must face the same challenges, achieve the same successes, in her story as you do in your own life.

The Silhouette reader is not afraid to enjoy herself. She knows when to take things seriously and when to indulge in a fantasy world. With six books a month, Silhouette Desire strives to meet her many moods, but each book is always a compelling love story.

Make a commitment to romance—go wild with Silhouette Desire!

Best,

Isabel Swift
Senior Editor & Editorial Coordinator

LAURIE PAIGE
Golden Promise

Silhouette Desire

Published by Silhouette Books New York

America's Publisher of Contemporary Romance

SILHOUETTE BOOKS
300 East 42nd St., New York, N.Y. 10017

Copyright © 1988 by Olivia M. Hall

ISBN: 0-373-05404-1

First Silhouette Books printing February 1988

America's Publisher of Contemporary Romance

Printed in the U.S.A.

Books by Laurie Paige

Silhouette Romance

South of the Sun #296
A Tangle of Rainbows #333
A Season for Butterflies #364
Nothing Lost #382
The Sea at Dawn #398

Silhouette Desire

Gypsy Enchantment #123
Journey to Desire #195
Golden Promise #404

Silhouette Special Edition

Lover's Choice #170

LAURIE PAIGE

has recently moved to California, where she is busy writing and falling off mountains—translation: trying to snow ski. During the summer she and her husband went camping, and she did a lot of falling there, too. Friends had brought along a Windsurfer, and she had to try it. As soon as she recovers from all this fun, she plans to use the information gained for some spunky heroine, who will be able to do each of them flawlessly on the second try!

For Lisa, who asked for it,
and Cindy, who didn't

One

Cynthia Robards cast a sympathetic glance at the name on the letter of her next postal stop. She didn't consider herself a bleeding heart, and certainly she wasn't psychic, but she knew what the man was doing here in the wild, rugged mountains of Idaho: he was licking his wounds.

Connor O'Shaugnessy was a man who had been hurt and had retreated to the wilderness until he was ready to face the world again on his own terms. She didn't blame him for seeking solitude at the old Taylor homestead on a fork of French Creek. It would have been her choice of location to recover from the wounds of life, too.

Banking the small amphibious plane in order to make the landing approach, she brought the light craft down on a smooth cove off the main waterway. She bumped the pier gently and, grabbing the painter, jumped out and tied up.

Glancing around, she frowned slightly. Usually, whenever residents heard the plane, they dropped what they were doing and dashed out to greet her. She was their life-line to civilization.

No one ran out to meet her from the old Taylor shack, which wasn't a shack anymore. Connor O'Shaugnessy had put in some hard work on the place. It looked like the perfect mountain retreat. She stared at it in amazement and delight.

New wood shingles covered the exterior. Broken windows that had been boarded over for years had been repaired, the glass replaced and the trim painted an attractive barn red. The sagging front porch had been rebuilt, with a new railing installed around it. The house looked inviting, and she ran lightly up the path.

When no one appeared at the open front door in answer to her call, she peered anxiously through the wire screen into the large living room.

Where was O'Shaugnessy? Was he in the woods? Possibly hurt? Probably not—she always thought the worst, she reminded herself honestly. She would look around and see if she could find him. If not, she would leave his letter on the kitchen table and be off.

She hoped he was in the vicinity. Something smelled wonderful in the cabin—stew or pot roast. And if she was not mistaken, fresh bread had been baked that morning. Her mouth watered, and she realized she was hungry.

Going around the outside of the house, she couldn't help but notice that the wind-blown debris had been cleared from the surrounding area and the wildflowers—white and yellow field daisies, purple lupine and orange paint-brush—had pushed up through the soil. Hundreds of bees hovered busily over the colorful meadow that sloped down to the creek. She paused for a second to soak up the sun and the breeze and the quiet bliss.

When she caught the muted sound of an ax on wood, she walked around the house, following the rhythmic thuds to an old shed several yards behind the main cabin.

O'Shaugnessy was using a tree stump as a base to stand the logs on in order to split them into halves, then quarters. Off to the side, several cords were neatly stacked, indicating his preparations for a long stay.

She stopped a safe distance from the flying chips and watched, spellbound, as he continued his chore. He was even more magnificent in person than he had been on television.

What had appeared on the news shows to be dark brown hair was now a deep red, with fiery highlights reflecting in the sun like embers in a hearth. Threads of reddish gold mingled with the darker strands.

He had laid his shirt aside and was wearing an old pair of tan cords. Each time he raised the ax high over his head muscles rippled beneath his skin. The breadth of his shoulders and the obvious strength in his arms and chest were impressive.

His rib cage rose in a graceful arch over his stomach, which dipped into a slightly concave curve with each lift of the ax. The skin on his back was tanned and smooth, glistening with the sweat of his labor. His chest was emphasized by the curling thatch of dark hair that formed a rough triangle from his throat to a point just above the clinging jeans.

For the first time in her life, she wanted to touch a man. The desire was so strong, she ached with the need. Her fingers curled tightly as she ignored the urge to run her hands along the exciting sinewy length of his torso.

What would he do if she did? Would he turn, look at her, lay the ax aside and take her into his arms? Would he carry her to the shady spot at the edge of the woods and make love to her there? Or would he take her into the re-constructed cabin?

Her breath stuck in her throat. What an odd fancy to be having in the bright light of noon! she chided her run-away imagination. And if *he* knew what had been on her mind, what would he think?

She smiled to herself. He would probably run for his life, sure that she was insane at the very least and perhaps dangerous. Besides, she had seen the type of woman he went for; his former fiancée had been a dashing brunette, small and full-figured.

Most men, much to her chagrin, treated her like a kid sister, bestowing on her the same warm, familial affection that her brother did. She had accepted long ago that she would never be a femme fatale, but she had always harbored the secret dream of being swept off her feet by some handsome devil who wouldn't be able to resist her charms, such as they were.

She was definitely the sweet and wholesome type. Her looks were presentable, but not overwhelming. No man would ever take one look and go off the deep end over her, she admitted, but there was no use in moaning about what wasn't to be.

Her attention was reclaimed by O'Shaugnessy as he tossed two freshly split pieces of firewood on the pile and stuck the ax into the stump with one mighty whack. He turned and stopped abruptly.

She had wondered what color his eyes were. Now she saw that they were green, as green as malachite and just as hard.

They seemed to stare at each other for an eternity before he finally spoke.

"Who the hell are you?" he demanded. Two tiny frown lines formed between his dark brows, which were a sharp contrast to his red hair. His gaze was stony.

Her throat was suddenly clogged, and she had to swallow once before she could speak. Connor O'Shaugnessy was easily the most intimidating person she had ever met. He was six-and-a-half feet tall and looked every inch of it.

Rage radiated from him, and she stepped back. Advancing toward him wouldn't be wise, she knew, not unless he extended an invitation.

She remembered his face when he had walked out of the courthouse and his weeping fiancée had thrown herself into his arms. He had put the woman aside, not harshly but firmly, and had walked on—alone.

"Hi. I'm your postman." She flashed him her most engaging grin and earned a deeper scowl.

Glancing up at him from under the cover of her long, spiky lashes, she ruefully admitted that he showed no signs of being bowled over by her beauty, her wit—after that brilliant opening line—or her feminine presence. Perhaps it was best that way. If he ever again fell for a woman, the crash would be heard clear over to Buffalo Hump, she mused, picturing the high peak several miles to the north.

"I have a letter for you," she added, holding up her hand to show him. Connor O'Shaugnessy was definitely handsome, but at the moment, he reminded her of a grizzly who could wipe her out with one swipe of his powerful hand.

No, he wouldn't, she reconsidered, remembering how gentle he had been with his former love the second time the news cameras had caught them together, immediately after the trial. How had he felt at that moment? Triumphant? Angry? Or merely tired of the whole mess? He had shown no emotion whatsoever.

He'd shown no mercy once his love had been forsaken; that had been quite clear when he had moved the petite woman aside. Did he still love her? Probably—he didn't seem like one who would change his mind, or heart, at the drop of a hat.

Cynthia couldn't help but feel wretched for him. He had been desperately hurt, his professional judgment called into question, his integrity denounced and his engagement ring thrown in his face, all on national television. It had been a terrible ordeal. He was entitled to some privacy and a time to heal.

She held out the letter to him, her gaze kind and sympathetic.

He walked over to her with a long, smooth stride and took it from her hand, glancing at the address on the front. "I suppose you know who I am," he said, looking resigned but sounding just like the prosecuting attorney at his trial.

Some of her compassion dried up at his unfriendly tone. "Yes. Connor O'Shaugnessy. I have to read the name in order to deliver the mail." She gave him a playful smile that suggested he relax.

The fine hair at her temples blew in wisps around her face as she gazed up at him. She caught the strands and pushed them back, unafraid of the glowering male, although he dominated her in size and strength.

He stuck the letter into his hip pocket without opening it. Usually she waited while her clients rushed through the contents of their mail, so anxious were they for news of home, before they sat down to talk to her. She was always invited in for a meal or snack before she went on her way.

"I'll put a box up at the end of the pier," he announced without so much as a thank-you for the letter. "Next time you can just stick my mail in it."

"I don't mind delivering it in person," she assured him.
"I like to check up on everyone, make sure you have
everything you need—I bring groceries and supplies as well
as the mail. Just give me a week's notice—"

"I won't need anything," he cut her off incisively.

"Oh." She nibbled thoughtfully on her lower lip for a
second, then glanced at her watch. "It's noon. I usually eat
lunch at your pier...." She paused and waited for him to
invite her in for lunch. When he didn't, she met his direct
stare with equanimity, refusing to be cowed by his unwelcoming regard. The situation was almost funny—she eager to stay, he impatient for her to be off.

Her curiosity and interest rose with his rejection. She
tried to suppress her natural concern for a fellow human,
but she couldn't help but worry about someone who so
obviously needed help.

His fiancée should have been with him, Cynthia
thought, angry at the woman for her lack of faith. She
should have stood by him during the hearings, instead of
running out on him, then wanting to come back as soon as
he had been vindicated. He had endured the trial alone.

According to the facts that had come out during the
sensational court case, he was an orphan who had worked
his way through college, graduating with high honors in
engineering and accepting a position with the prestigious
construction and development firm of Babs, Claymore and
Barker.

After several successful years with the company, he had
been promoted to general manager when Babs, Claymore
and Barker had been bought out by a larger firm. Shortly
after he'd settled into his new job, a bridge had collapsed
two days after its scaffolding had been dismantled. Three
workman had been seriously injured: one might never walk
again. Connor O'Shaugnessy had been arrested for sub-

stituting inferior material for the more expensive kind
called for in the specifications and for taking a kickback
from the supplier.

After a year and a half of investigation, and a lengthy
trial, he had been found innocent. His detectives discovered that the boss's son, the brother of Connor's fiancée,
had been the one who had changed the orders, pocketed
the difference and altered the records so the blame would
fall on Connor.

Cynthia thought of that long period when he had been
out of work and without friends. He had withstood it all
without cracking once, at least not while the cameras were
on him.

Tears filled her eyes. A strong man like that deserved a
strong woman, one who would have stood by him.

"Can't you find another place?" he asked.

"Another place for what . . . oh, for lunch." She suddenly remembered the topic of discussion. "I was hoping
you would invite me to eat with you," she said, tilting her
head to one side. "I smelled something delicious when I
peeked in the door."

She had decided he needed a friend, someone to talk to
while he worked out his bitterness. She would have to be
that person; there was no one else within miles.

"I'm usually here by noon every Tuesday and Friday,"
she continued. "On Fridays, I stay with my brother, who's
operating an old mine farther up the river." She pointed in
the general direction.

Connor hooked his thumbs into his front pockets. "This
is Friday. Why don't you have lunch with him?"

Cynthia laughed. "For one thing, he's a terrible cook—
even worse than I am. For another, he'll be down in his
mine." She waited expectantly.

"Too bad," he said, and turned his back. He disappeared into the shed and left her standing there, still waiting for him to extend an invitation to her.

Feeling that she had walked into that situation with her eyes open, she retraced her steps to the pier and started to climb into the plane. She didn't need an order to depart; the insult of his turned back had been quite enough. A bit more of her compassion faded—a large bit.

Forever stubborn, she decided that instead of leaving she would eat lunch on his pier in spite of his desire to be rid of her. After all, she had been eating there every Tuesday and Friday for two years, weather permitting. That ought to give her squatter's rights, she decided, glancing over her shoulder at the house as she retrieved a small cooler from the plane.

He was standing on his front porch, watching her.

She was startled by his presence and direct stare, but she smiled gamely and waved. She plunked herself down on the wooden pier and dangled her legs over the edge while she fished her sandwich out of its plastic bag and pulled the tab on a can of lemonade.

Leaning over the water, she studied her face while she chewed meditatively on her lunch. Her hair formed soft spirals around her face, having long ago escaped the barrettes at her temples. Thick and baby-fine, it was the bane of her life; she could spend hours putting it up, only to have it fall down while she was still before the mirror.

Relaxing against a thick piling, she sighed deeply and tried to let the surrounding peace and tranquillity penetrate her soul as it usually did. It didn't work; she was too aware of the man behind her.

He had thought she was an illusion, standing there in the sunlight with the wind teasing her honey-brown hair into tangled curls around her face. Her shirt was pastel pink and covered her body lightly—her shoulders, the gentle protrusion of her breasts, the flare of her jeans-clad hips.

For a long moment, he had been unable to speak but had gazed at her with a longing that had been almost overpowering. She had been sent to him, and he wanted to take her, to claim her as his compensation for all the months of anger and frustration, and for the loneliness that had never gone away.

When Veronica had come into his life, he had thought his single years were over. He became part of her clan—or thought he had. As soon as there had been trouble, the Trennon family—father, son and daughter—had closed ranks, and he had been the odd man out. It was a lesson he wasn't likely to forget.

Just as he wasn't going to forget and let himself be drawn into any kind of involvement with that enticing— and stubborn—female who now sat on his dock and ate her lunch, defying his attempts to get rid of her. In his mental vision, he saw her again as he had when he looked up from splitting logs.

She had said nothing, had just watched him, her eyes a beautiful golden amber, with incredibly long lashes. Her gaze had been kind. It wasn't until he had realized she knew who he was—the whole sorry story had been splashed across state and national headlines for months— that he had felt the return of the old, familiar anger, an emotion he had found useful as a defense against a world that had tried to intrude on his private life, his thoughts, even his hopes and dreams.

He was reluctantly amused at her impulsive defiance. She had started to climb into her plane, then had changed her mind, obviously deciding to enjoy her lunch on his pier in spite of his earlier rudeness.

However, anger still boiled his blood, although he couldn't figure out why. Perhaps he resented her fresh-faced innocence, as if she still believed in the good things in life. Or, more realistically, he simply didn't want to be bothered with her.

He had come here to rest and be alone, away from hounding reporters, a sobbing ex-fiancée and an apologetic ex-boss who had said some pretty nasty things until it came out that his own son was the culprit. Who needed them? He didn't need anyone, especially a do-gooder parading as a friendly everyday flying postman.

He picked up his toolbox and the rough mailbox he had just assembled in the shed and brought them down to the pier, where she sat eating a sandwich with her back braced against a piling and her feet kicking over the side of the dock.

The wind ruffled her hair, bringing more disorder to the unruly spirals at the sides of her face and the curls cascading around her shoulders. Her hair was tantalizingly beautiful, although she didn't seem to make much use of the fact.

Still, with eyes like hers, didn't she realize that no man who looked into them would be safe from her? A rueful grimace flashed across his face as he acknowledged his own attraction to them.

He glanced along the pier as he stepped onto the wooden structure. This woman obviously didn't use her assets the way most of her sex did, as temptations to lure a man into her web. She was more subtle with her come-laugh-with-me eyes and challenging smile.

He shook his head as if to clear the harsh thoughts. For some reason, his friendly postlady didn't seem to deserve them. She looked too pure, too innocent, to be compared with Veronica and her sophisticated friends.

The loneliness must be getting to him more than he had realized. These crazy thoughts had to go.

Glancing away from her, he picked up a couple of large nails and the hammer and pounded the wooden box into position on top of the corner piling. Then he opened and closed the makeshift door to see if the rusty hinges worked.

"There. You can leave the mail in the box from now on." He took a perverse delight in making the statement; he wouldn't have to see her again or hear that burbling laughter underscoring her voice.

She looked up at him, her eyes seeming to glow with a penetrating warmth. He hardened his heart against the unexpected turbulence that grew until he was filled with a strong aching need to touch her, hold her, know the comfort of her arms....

The muscles of his strong, squared-off jaw knotted as he clenched his teeth and stalked off.

Cynthia watched him as his ground-clearing stride took him swiftly back to the cabin. He had obviously been angry that his privacy had been invaded, but she hadn't been able to identify the other emotions in his jade-green eyes. What had he been thinking in that second before he had abruptly left her?

Staring into the water of the tiny cove, she absently took another bite of her sandwich. With a grimace at the lunch meat spread liberally with mustard between the two pieces of rye bread, she thought of the meal he had on the stove. A wide grin curved over her lips. She should march right up to the door and demand to be fed, but maybe he didn't have much food or a lot of money.

This new worry caused her to frown. She would have to keep an eye on him in spite of his obvious wish to be alone. He had been by himself for eighteen months; that was quite enough time in hibernation. Very gradually, she would win his trust and friendship, then introduce him to the other residents of the mountains.

Because they seldom saw one another, most of the homesteaders and solitary miners were interested in their isolated neighbors. Their desire for a simpler existence created a bond that was strengthened by the occasional get-together for a house-raising or welcoming party. She would see that Connor O'Shaugnessy knew of these happenings.

He was lonely, she thought, but he didn't want to admit it. People needed people, and he was no different from anyone else. She would wait. Sooner or later, all men confided in her as if she were their favorite sister.

She sighed as she got up and put her empty sandwich bag and lemonade can in the cooler. With other men, it hadn't mattered so much, but with this one . . . she didn't want to be his sister. . . .

Two

Cynthia buzzed the small meadow near her brother's cabin to make sure there were no animals on it, then set the plane down lightly on the grass. She stretched and yawned as she climbed the slope to the two-room log house, lugging a small weekend case with her. She was filled with a sense of homecoming.

She loved this country—all of it, from the Bitterroot Mountains in the east, which formed part of the Continental Divide, to the Hells Canyon of the Snake River, which plunged to a depth of 7,900 feet to the canyon floor and extended 125 miles along the Oregon border.

Originally from Portland, she had worked out of Boise for two years now, after bidding on and winning the contract to deliver mail to some of the remote regions of the national forests.

As children, she and Adam had loved to come here and stay with their uncle, a hermit who had built the compact

A-frame structure, then worked an abandoned mine for gold. Oddly, a bag of gold nuggets had been found in Uncle Abbot's cabin after his death, but no other finds had been reported in the area since the original strike, back in the 1800s. Everyone wondered where he had found those pieces of gold.

As she had expected, her brother wasn't in when she entered the cabin. She dumped her carryall on the bunk bed and returned to the plane to bring in the groceries.

That finished, she cubed a roast, dredged it with flour, browned it in a big iron pot and added vegetables to make beef stew. She and Adam would have to eat crackers with their meal; homemade bread was beyond her talent.

"But my stew will be as good as yours, Mr. O'Shaugnessy," she declared two hours later as she tasted it.

"Talking to yourself? That's the first sign," Adam said, walking in the open door and closing it behind him. The sun was going down, and the night air was rapidly cooling off. "How was the trip?" he added, his grimy face split into a grin.

"Fine." She silently appraised him while he washed up and she dished out the stew. He looked good.

His light brown hair had grown a lot since his last haircut and clung to his neck and face in stray curls. His eyes, blue flecked with amber, looked peaceful. He was more than happy; he was content. Coming here had been a wise decision for him.

"How about giving me a haircut?" he requested, pulling at a stray lock. "I can't stand it in my face while I work."

"Okay. After supper?"

"Um-hmm. Something smells delicious." He hung the towel on the rack and took his seat at the table. Reaching across, he absently ruffled the flyaway curls on her forehead. "You really outdid yourself this time."

"I probably left the salt out," she said, declaiming her culinary talents, which ran to the very simple.

He lifted the fork to his mouth and savored one first morsel. "No, you got it down to a science this time. I knew you could do it if you kept practicing."

"You can write me up a commendation," she responded to his teasing. He had often told her she had to improve her cooking if she expected to get a man. "The stomach is still the way to the heart," he had superciliously explained more than once after eating her less-than-successful endeavors.

They ate their dinner in companionable silence, not resuming the conversation until the table was cleared and their few dishes were washed and dried.

"Who were you arguing with when I came in?" Adam asked as he took his seat and let her place a towel around his neck.

She ran a comb through his hair, which wasn't as curly as hers but was as thick, and began the task of trimming it into shape. "Your new neighbor down on the next fork of the creek. His name is Connor O'Shaugnessy."

Adam repeated the name. "Haven't I heard of him?"

"Uh-hmm. Don't you remember the article on him in the Sunday magazine section a few months ago? He was the engineer—"

"On the bridge that collapsed in San Francisco right after they got it up. I remember now."

"Yes, well, he's retreated to the old Taylor place to lick his wounds."

"Uh-oh," Adam said, brushing at the loose hair that had fallen over his face.

"Be still. What does 'uh-oh' mean?" she demanded. She held up a strand between two fingers and clipped the ends off.

"Another lame duck," he explained dryly. "Another lonely soul so injured by life that you, my dear sister, will feel compelled to take him under your wing until you're sure he's healed and ready to return to the fray. You haven't gotten rid of Mr. Taylor yet."

She laughed. "This one is no duck—more like a bear with a sore paw. He's fierce."

There was a thoughtful pause. "You're attracted to him," her brother concluded, bringing a grimace to her mobile lips.

"Don't move, or I'll snip your ear," she warned. Carefully, she trimmed around each ear until the thick locks feathered smoothly away from his temples, then she finished layering the back until it just touched his collar. "There, that's better," she declared as she removed the towel and brushed off his neck and face.

"I'll go take a quick shower," he decided, standing and stretching lazily to his full six-foot height.

Cynthia thought of Connor's lanky frame, of the way his jeans had clung to his lean hips, of his trim waist, which emphasized the breadth of his shoulders. She pictured the thick cords of muscle that had rippled so sinuously under his deeply tanned skin. A redhead who tans, she thought, realizing that she hadn't noticed any freckles.

But then, she hadn't seen all of him, she admitted, laughter brightening her amber eyes. The amusement disappeared abruptly as she contemplated the possibility. She imagined those broad, capable hands on her, caressing her with gentle passion.

Lost in a daydream, she didn't notice Adam's perplexed stare, his slight shrug at her obvious absentmindedness and his departure to the bathroom at the back of the cabin. She saw dark red hair with fiery highlights and eyes like green gems shining down on her as she lay on a bearskin rug....

Her heart pounding like a startled deer's, Cynthia added more wood to the fire and settled in an old-fashioned rocking chair with a cane bottom. She knew the layout of Connor's house. She had been in it many times before last fall, when Mr. Taylor's family had insisted he go to a nursing home in Boise. The cabin had stood empty and forlorn during the winter, and as a result of a heavy work-load that spring, she had returned only intermittently for her solitary picnics.

There was a fireplace in the main room of the house, she recalled, and a wide archway opening into the cozy kitchen. The range was fueled by gas, and she wondered how the tank was replenished. Connor must have had the outside road repaired in order to get a truck over it; Mr. Taylor had let it go until it was almost impassable.

When she had peered in the door, she had noticed the furniture was different from what she remembered. Connor had certainly put a lot of work into the house, and if the pile of firewood was any indication, he had every intention of staying through the winter at the very least.

Sighing worriedly, Cynthia thought of the effects of total solitude on a man who had been deceived. It would be a terrible waste for Connor to become embittered and withdrawn. Instinctively, she knew he had a lot to offer in the way of friendship and loyalty—and, to the right woman, a great deal of love.

He would be demanding as a lover; he would want the total love and trust of his partner. But would he give the same? Not if he let himself stay up in the mountains with hatred growing in his heart.

Driven by a desire stronger than her common sense, she had to see that that didn't happen. Deep within that fierce exterior was a heart that beat as gently as any that had ever existed.

Rubbing a towel over his wet hair, Adam came into the room and pulled a chair close to the stove. At his sister's fleeting grin, he frowned. "What's up with you and this guy down the river?"

Startled at his tone, Cynthia shook her head. "Nothing." A long pause followed as she turned away from her brother. "I am worried about him," she admitted finally. "I don't think he should be alone in his condition. He's too...too vulnerable." The word didn't seem to fit Connor but it was the only one she could think of.

"Listen, Cyn, mind your own business. You don't know anything about the man except what you read in the papers." Adam snorted in disgust. "You read that he's an orphan, so all right, I'll concede he had a hard life. Other people do, too. Don't go wasting your pity on somebody you know nothing about."

"Adam—"

"He didn't do anything criminal, but for all we know, he may be a fortune hunter who was after the main chance with the daughter of a rich man. Have you thought of that?"

Her shocked expression said she hadn't.

"See? You always expect the best from people and never suspect anyone of ulterior motives. I wish you could find someone worthy of you. He'd be a lucky son of a gun," Adam declared.

Cynthia laid a soothing hand on his arm. Her baby brother, fifteen months younger than she, was concerned about her, and she loved him for it. However, that didn't solve the problem.

She realized she already thought of Connor O'Shaugnessy by his first name, as if they were friends. Having kept up with the accounts of his trial, she felt she had known him for ages, known him and liked him.

"Don't worry. I'm not about to fall for that red-haired grouch. But he could use a friend. It's no more than a two-hour walk. If you were ever over that way, you could drop in, couldn't you?"

Adam rolled his eyes heavenward. "When would I ever be over that way?" he asked with precise logic.

She gestured impatiently. "You never know when you might feel like a Sunday stroll."

"Yeah, over a mountain ridge and down a ravine," he scoffed. "Don't get involved with him, Cyn."

At the suddenly serious tone, she looked at Adam. He met her gaze levelly. "Why?" she asked quietly.

"Because I have a hunch that he would hurt you. You're already half in love with him and you just met him."

"Love! That's ridiculous. I hardly know him, except for what I've seen on TV and read in the papers. It's just that—"

Adam ruffled her hair. "I know. That big, generous heart of yours can't stand for anyone to be unhappy. Don't you think it might be good for him to be alone for a while? You thought it was fine for me, even supported me for two years," he added wryly.

She smiled warmly at him. "The circumstances were different. You needed to get out of the fast track and away from your high-living friends in Portland. Your leaving was in the nature of a strategic retreat; Connor's is a withdrawal. Do you see the difference?"

"Connor, is it?" he drawled.

Her gaze dropped to her lap. "I think of him that way. He's going to be my friend...whether he knows it or not!" She looked up with a defiant, laughing sparkle in her eyes.

Her brother studied her set expression, and threw back his head and laughed heartily. Cynthia made a face at him; her statement hadn't been that funny.

"I can see it now," Adam declared when he finally regained his composure. "The battle between David and Goliath. And we all know what happened to the giant, don't we?"

"He got beaned on the head—the same thing that's going to happen to you if you don't stop the insinuations," she warned.

"Get out the cards," Adam ordered, then rose and poured two mugs of strong coffee, thus ending the discussion for the present. Maybe he would take a walk across the ridge some Sunday and check out this O'Shaugnessy fellow. "I've got a new game."

"You said that last time." She shuffled the deck and started dealing. She and her brother had conducted an ongoing game of rummy for a year. Neither would agree to quit as long as the other was winning. "What's the score?"

"8,602 to 8,528, your favor."

"Let's quit," she promptly suggested.

"Not on your life," he snapped, turning his chair to the table and picking up the opening hand.

Later, when Adam was sound asleep in his bunk, Cynthia thought of his concern about her involvement with Connor. Not that there was an involvement, but if one developed... No, it was silly to even think about it.

She tried to go to sleep, but it was no use. She kept seeing the way Connor had almost smiled when she had waved at him. She would like to see a full smile on his face, to hear a hearty laugh.

Outside, an owl hooted; the sound was as lonely as the night.

Was Connor lying in his bed, listening to the night and thinking of his future? What was it about him that called to some deep, inner part of her? Adam was afraid she would get hurt if she got mixed up with Connor, but just thinking of him made her ache to hold him and comfort him. She had never felt this way before. It was the oddest thing....

Connor glanced at the sun's position for the tenth time in the last twenty minutes. Where was she?

He remembered in detail what she had looked like as she had stood and watched him chop wood. The sun had highlighted the thick waves in her hair and sparkled in her eyes. She had been fairly tall and slender, her pink shirt giving only a hint of the figure beneath. But it had been enough to send his imagination into overtime in the four days since she'd delivered the letter from his lawyer.

He smiled sardonically. The envelope had contained a check for all the back pay he had missed, plus a hefty damage settlement, negotiated out of court in return for his dropping his countersuit for damages against his former boss. With that and his investments, he could afford to live here for the rest of his life.

Her gaze had been gentleness itself, revealing sympathy in the crystalline depths as if she knew exactly what he had gone through. He frowned darkly. His agony wasn't going to be shared with anyone, he thought fiercely.

Besides, he had long ago gotten over any feelings induced by the events of the last year and a half. He was at peace with himself; he had fought the battle and won. Now it was over.

For several minutes, he tried to ignore the need to check the sun's position. It was no use. Where was she? Hadn't she said she ate lunch on the dock every Tuesday and Friday? Today was Tuesday.

Maybe she stopped only when she had a letter to deliver. He wasn't expecting any mail except for an occasional note from Brad, his attorney, who had become his friend. But the old man who had lived here had been gone for months, and she had indicated that she had still landed and had her solitary picnic.

He glanced up. One or one-thirty, by the sun.

He gave in to several conflicting feelings—annoyance that she hadn't arrived when she said she would, irritation at the memory of her defiance. Having made it plain that he'd wanted her gone, she had sat herself down on the end of the pier and had eaten her lunch. Obviously, she knew nothing about his temper.

When was the last time he had done anything rash, just for the hell of it?

Nothing came to mind. His mother had died when he was five, and from the time his father had dropped him at the children's home when he was nine, he had planned his life—now he was going to escape and become somebody important, somebody who was respected.

He remembered the matron's words when she opened the door. "Oh, no, another one, Sister Barnabas. Where shall we put him?" She hadn't meant to be unkind; they had had their hands full, running a house overflowing with unwanted boys. He had grown to love Barney before she had been transferred to another orphanage.

The sun continued to move across the sky.

He went back to work. His project was to remodel the shed into a stable to shelter his horse and pack mule. He needed the animals for trips to the general store over the old logging road, which he didn't intend to repair; the rough terrain would discourage visitors.

The sunlight gleaming on a bit of tack reminded him of the color of her eyes. Golden. Pure amber. Dammit, stop thinking about her eyes. They were just eyes; everybody had eyes. But hers had been soft, gentle . . . pitying.

He gritted his teeth. He didn't need pity, either.

Where the hell was she?

The sound of a plane's engine brought such a flood of relief that he nearly dropped the saw. Fury immediately followed. She was getting to him, and he didn't like it, not one little bit. He didn't need anybody, especially not little Miss Sweetness-and-Light.

He determinedly went on with his task after the engine was cut and silence again descended on the homestead. He strained to catch any sound of her activities, but could hear only the drone of bees and the whisper of the wind.

She was probably eating her sandwich and dangling her legs over the pier, knowing it irritated him no end for her to be on his property. Finally, he threw down his saw and stalked around to the front of the cabin. She was just closing the crude mailbox.

"Junk mail," she called in a friendly tone.

He did a slow burn. Didn't she know enough to understand he had deliberately insulted her last Friday? Didn't she know she wasn't wanted? He looked at the tilt of her chin. Of course she did. He ought to go down there and . . . and . . .

Cynthia got her lunch out of the plane and sat down in her favorite place. The water had risen quite a bit as the warm spring sun melted the snow on the higher peaks.

Settling back with her sandwich and a can of lemonade, she smiled, amused with her mixed emotions from last Friday.

Over the past few days, she had regained her equilibrium and could view her emotional turbulence, which had been induced by her fierce, antisocial postal patron, with the nonchalance it deserved.

Adam was right about her propensity for taking people under her wing. He had reminded her of the time a fellow employee had been accused of stealing and she had taken his side, only to discover he really had been guilty.

"But Connor was proven innocent," she had protested. "And he needs help. His trust in mankind has been damaged."

"Darn it, Cyn, it isn't your place to patch up every wounded human you come in contact with!" Adam had exploded.

She shook her head slightly. Poor Adam. He was worried about her getting hurt, but she didn't expect anything from people that they didn't want to give. She hadn't realized how responsible Adam felt toward her, probably because he was the reason for her being here. Occasionally he expressed guilt over that; however, she was quite content with her life.

She had been only too happy to get him away from the city. At college, with too much money and too much freedom, he had fallen in with a fast crowd, friends who thought life was a lark and who would try anything once. When he'd earned failing grades and had been kicked out of school, he had come to her rather than return home in disgrace.

Remembering how much she and Adam had enjoyed their summers with their Uncle Abbott, she had suggested he come to Idaho and try his hand at mining. That had been a wise move.

A noise behind her brought her head around with a quick jerk, disrupting her retrospection.

Connor O'Shaugnessy stood on the dock with a sawn plank balanced between his two hands. On the makeshift tray were a steaming bowl, a plate covered with a neckerchief, and a tall glass of milk. "Lunch," he said without so much as the hint of a smile touching the chiseled lines of his hard mouth.

"If it offends you so much to bring it, why bother?" she asked. She was at once ashamed of herself. Here he was, obviously trying to make amends for last week, and she was acting like a shrew.

"It doesn't offend me. Do you want it or not?"

"Yes," she said in a calmer voice. "Where did you get the fresh milk?"

He placed the plank across her lap after she held her arms up out of the way. "It's the kind you can keep on the shelf for months."

Cynthia stared at the big bowl of beef stew. She peeked under the cloth—warm bread spread with butter. Her stomach gave a loud growl of approval, and she couldn't resist laughing.

"Won't you join me?" she invited him.

He hesitated, shook his head and stalked over to the mailbox. He got out the advertisement, which was addressed to "Resident" and had a box number and rural route number on it, and retreated up the path.

She observed the swing of his powerful shoulders until he was gone, then she threw her baloney sandwich to the fish, picked up the neckerchief, laid it over her knees, and began to eat.

The stew was as good as it smelled, just as she had known it would be. Connor O'Shaugnessy wasn't a man to do something less than perfectly. She knew that just as surely as the sun rose over the Bitterroot Mountains.

Just as she was scooping up the last drop of stew with the last bite of bread, he returned. He came out on the short dock, set a piece of cherry pie down beside her and settled himself a few feet away, his back against a stout piling. Lifting a fork, he began to eat the dessert.

"Do you want some more milk?" he asked.

His voice was gruff, but not unfriendly. She refused his offer with a smile and picked up the fork and plate of pie.

"This is delicious. Did you make it? Or do you have a staff working overtime to produce all this?" Her gesture took in the pile of dirty dishes.

"I put it together, but the ingredients came from a can," he told her.

"Mmm," she murmured in understanding.

They were silent after they finished eating, watching the play of sunlight on the water. Cynthia noticed a trace of sawdust along one leg of his jeans and on his jogging shoes, then noted the freshly cut plank that he had served her lunch on. His thoughtfulness warmed her.

"Thank you very much for lunch," she said softly. "I'm sorry I was hateful earlier."

He looked surprised. "It was nothing."

He wasn't used to people apologizing to him when they hurt his feelings, she mused. He seemed hard on the outside, but he had been terribly hurt. She felt sad and angry for him.

Connor glanced at her when she sighed audibly. What was she thinking, sitting there so lost in her thoughts? He wasn't a man given to probing into other people's motives, but he found himself wondering about hers. Her lashes hid her eyes as she stared at the water lapping against the dock, but to him she seemed sad.

Connor O'Shaugnessy, the great analyzer of the female psyche. He had been wrong about women before; he wasn't going to start reading anything into this one that wasn't there.

She looked over at him, meeting his gaze with a candor and openness that seemed to let him look clear into her soul. Again he was caught in her charm. He wanted something from her, something so powerful it scared him. Drawing a shaky breath, he forced himself to look away.

He had better watch it. She would be his only contact with the outside world. It would be easy for him to imagine that he needed her. If he wanted company, the letter from Brad had indicated his willingness to come visit for a few days and get some fishing in, if Connor was ready for guests. He wasn't.

"The River of No Return," she said in a low, dreamy voice after a few minutes.

"What?" His voice sounded husky to his ears. He cleared it gruffly, angry and unnerved by his lack of control. What was she to him that he was letting her get under his skin this way? Nothing. Not a damned thing.

"The Salmon River," she explained. "It was called the 'River of No Return' by the early trappers and mountain men. It flows west and is so rough and wild, there's no way to return along it."

She thought of traveling the river with Connor. To go with him would be an adventure, a wild ride down a river of golden dreams that led to love. And there would be no going back for either of them, not ever....

"There was a movie by that name." He tried to recall it.

"Robert Mitchum and Marilyn Monroe," she confirmed promptly. "He carried her off with him at the end.

Do you remember? And she lost one of her red satin shoes in the muddy street, but she didn't care. She was going with her man.''

"The fantasy ending," he scoffed.

She stared down the creek. She knew that a few miles downstream it joined the Salmon, which flowed into the Snake River, which became part of the Columbia, which eventually rushed into the Pacific. The ocean evaporated, became rain, which fell on the mountains, and the whole cycle was repeated. It seemed to indicate the continuity of life.

"I know you don't believe in it right now, but someday you will again." She spoke with conviction.

She sounded so sincere that he found himself almost believing her. Next thing he knew, he'd be spouting poems. He wanted this woman with the glowing eyes. She was beautiful, and it had been a long time since he had been in the company of a woman with this much allure.

Glancing at the dreamy expression on her kittenish face, he hardened his heart. "Yeah," he said bitingly, "dance hall girl finds true love and lives happily ever after as a farmer's wife."

Cynthia refused to take offense. It was enough for now that he was even talking to her. The fact that he was, indicated his need to do so. She'd been right.

She felt an unbidden deep tenderness for him. Adam would be furious with her. He thought she was too soft-hearted, that people took advantage of her, but it wasn't true. She liked people, and she didn't mind sharing her enthusiasm with them.

"Well, I'd better get on the road," she said after several minutes of tense silence. An inexplicable attraction existed between them, she realized when she met his eyes.

Goose bumps raced along her spine as she recognized raw hunger in his gaze. Heat spread through her veins, pulsing with each beat of her heart. She experienced again that aching need to touch him that she had first felt when she'd watched him chopping wood.

She stood abruptly, awkwardly, as if to make an escape. "I'd better go," she repeated, suddenly nervous.

"Yes," he agreed, standing and gazing down at her. "Yes, you'd better run." His slight smile was sardonic.

She was shocked that he had read her so well.

"I've seen your kind before." His eyes darkened in anger. "At the orphanage. They would come at Christmas and Easter to bring gifts for the poor little homeless boys, all full of kindness and smiles. Then they would leave, having done their duty and their kind acts for the balance of the year."

"You're bitter," she stated. "More than I thought you would be, more than I had realized." It would be harder to reach him than she had thought; she refused to admit that it might be impossible. Everyone had a chink in his armor.

"I don't need your pity, postlady." He put his hands on his hips and defied her to feel sorry for him.

"I don't pity you," she said softly, disarming him with the simple truth. "You're a strong man, morally as well as physically. A lesser person wouldn't have handled your problems with such skill."

Thinking of his strength of character and innate gentleness, she felt these qualities shouldn't be lost to the world due to a cruel twist of fate. He had loved once—wrongly—but he could learn to trust again.

If she couldn't help him herself, then she would just have to find someone who could. The only problem was that he seemed to read her like a printed page.

Maybe Adam was right; maybe she had better stay away from this fierce, wounded warrior. He could find his own way back to civilization.

"Thanks for the vote of confidence." His smile was brief.

"I have to go," she said. "I'll try not to bother you again. If you do find you need something, just tie a red bandanna to the mailbox and put a note inside. I'll drop in, even if I don't have any mail for you."

"I expect I'll be fine," he said, evidently regretting that he had allowed himself to reveal so much to her.

"Good." She untied the ropes, tossed them inside, climbed into the light aircraft and started the engine.

"What's your name?" he called out.

"What?" She leaned out the door and watched his lips as he repeated the question.

"Your name. What's your name?"

"Cynthia Robards." She smiled slightly, not sure if his scowl meant he hadn't heard or that he had, but didn't like her name. A very moody bear, she decided. Waving, she closed the door, then taxied into position for takeoff.

"Cynthia," he repeated to himself as he watched the plane disappear behind the trees at the bend of the creek. "Cynthia," he said again in a low growl. "Cyn."

The name came easily to his lips, rolling off his tongue in a sibilant murmur. A sexy name to whisper when they made love.

He gathered the dishes and returned to the cabin. When he was inside, his eyes strayed to the old bearskin rug he had found in a closet. After a good beating and airing, it had been presentable enough to lay before the hearth. He could see her there with him, her hair like dark streams of honey flowing around them, her eyes gleaming like melted

butter from the heat of their union, his name on her lips,
soft and sweet. She would be so sweet.

His eyes turned hard. He wasn't going to get mixed up
with anyone. Peace and quiet, a time alone—those were
the things he wanted. And that was the way it would be.

Three

___

Cynthia listened to the beat of the plane's engine. Instead of a smooth, monotonous drone, it hummed a distinct rhythmic pattern, a sign of engine trouble. One of the cylinders was misfiring. There was one thing her flight instructor had impressed on her: when the engine acts up, get the plane on the ground. It was a lot easier to work on land than on a cloud.

Over the next ridge was Connor's place. She could land in the alcove and borrow Connor's truck to get the serum over to the Graceson family. She thought of Connor's piercing gaze. She didn't feel like meeting that silent wall of antipathy today. Maybe she could nurse the plane along; it wasn't that much farther to the other place.

Ignoring her own misgivings, she followed the curve of the narrow valley instead of going over the ridge. Five minutes later, she knew she had made a mistake. The engine coughed, spluttered and quit for a long second before catching again.

Using an updraft, she banked into a sweeping turn and let the wind lift her over the ridge as she chose a straight course to get to Connor's cabin. In a few minutes, she was tying up at his pier. Naturally, he didn't run out to say hello and get his mail; he never did.

During the past two weeks, she'd had mail for him twice. He hadn't put in an appearance either time. She had suppressed her concern; if something was wrong, he would have to come to her. She had refused to go looking for him.

After another few minutes of silence, she felt more than a passing irritation. She needed him. Where was he?

At that moment, he came around the house, running.

She stood there, spellbound. He looked wonderful—larger than life and twice as forceful. His hair gleamed like dark flames as he slowed to a jog. His chest was bare, the hair matted with perspiration as if he had been working hard.

He wore a pair of jogging shorts, and she couldn't help but notice the strength of the long, ropey muscles in his legs. He bounded over the uneven terrain and came to a stop before her.

"Are you all right?" he asked, his voice hoarse as he gasped for breath.

"Yes." She was mesmerized by the fire in his eyes as he surveyed her slender figure. His perusal didn't miss one particle.

Her skin felt as if it had been burned, and she trembled with the force of her reaction. She wanted to leap into his arms and feel him touch her, kiss her. She saw his hands clench into fists and imagined them on her, pulling her to his large frame, which was wiry and agile, like a professional athlete's. She looked away.

"I heard your engine quit," he said. "It was spluttering, then it quit."

Was that really worry in his eyes? she wondered. He had probably been afraid he would be inundated by rescue workers and reporters if she crashed on his property.

"Yes, fortunately I was already landing and could glide the rest of the way. I think one of my plugs is fouled...."

"Don't you check the damned thing out before you take off?" he questioned, practically snarling.

"Yes." Her reply was frosty. She didn't need a lecture from him on how to care for her equipment. "I need to use your truck," she said, more as an order than a request.

He looked perplexed. "I don't have a truck."

She shrugged as she turned to the plane and pulled out the package of serum. "Whatever you used to get here. I have serum to deliver."

"I don't have a vehicle," he told her. "What kind of serum?"

She ignored his question. "What do you mean you don't have a vehicle? How did you get all that building material up here in order to repair the cabin? How do you get down to the store to buy groceries?" She placed one hand on her hip as she glared up at him. He was standing very close to her, and she could see the rivulets of sweat running down his face and dripping onto his chest. He radiated heat.

"I had the stuff delivered by helicopter. I brought enough food to last the summer," he explained impatiently. "What's the serum for?" He took hold of her shoulders and gave her a little shake. "Snakebite? Who's been bitten?"

"Not bitten, stung. The Gracesons' nephew is visiting, and he got stung several times. He's having a severe reaction. I was asked to fly over to Lewiston and pick up some medicine." She glanced at the plane. "I'll have to try to get the engine fixed so I can get over there."

"I have a horse." At her glance of surprise he explained, "I use it and a pack mule to get down to the store when I need something. How far is the other house from here?"

"The next place down the logging road, just beyond the fork of the river," she told him. "Maybe I can figure out what's wrong with the plane. That would be faster—if it's something I can fix. Maybe I can find a spare spark plug," she ended on a hopeful note, her thoughts disjointed as she tried to figure out the best thing to do.

"I'd say it was more than a spark plug."

"Yes," she agreed glumly. "But it would take too long to go on foot."

"I said you could use my horse," he reminded her. "He can make it in an hour."

"I can't ride."

"Anybody can ride."

"Horses and I don't get along very well. One of them threw me, then had the audacity to trample on me." She tried to grin but failed. The episode with the stallion had been imprinted on her at age eight, and she had never forgotten her terror as the huge beast had turned on her, rearing again and again, his iron-clad hooves slashing the air above her.

Connor didn't say anything as she turned back toward the plane. He watched as she began checking out the engine with knowledge and skill. Reluctantly, he admitted to the admiration she obviously deserved. That wasn't the only reaction she aroused in him.

Watching her slender figure as she worked, he was reminded of the taunting desire he had lived with since he had first seen her. Never had a woman so completely taken possession of his thoughts and senses. She was dangerous....

"It's no use," she said in disgust. "It has to be the gas line. I don't have time to check it out." She eyed Connor speculatively. "You could ride your horse over. Do you know how to give shots?"

Connor held up both hands. "No, and I'm not about to learn on a kid."

"No, it would be too difficult, and possibly hazardous, if you don't know what you're doing." She thought desperately, but no solution came to mind. "I'll have to try to reach the ranger station and see if there's someone available with emergency medical training. And if the helicopter is in—"

"You can ride with me," he heard himself offer. "I'll hold you so you won't fall off." What was he letting himself in for?

Still, she hesitated. Glancing at the plane, then her watch, she gave up. "Let's go." She retrieved the package of medicine.

While Connor saddled up the brown horse, she stayed outside the gate. The horse and the man were both big and brawny, smooth and graceful. The stallion was beautiful and disciplined, but Cynthia was too nervous to heed his finer points.

Connor went in to change clothes, leaving the horse tied to the gate. In a few minutes, he came out with several items, which he stored in saddlebags. To these he added the package of serum. After tying a blanket roll behind the saddle, he led the horse out of the fenced area and vaulted into the saddle. He held out a hand to her as he slipped his foot from the stirrup.

"Maybe the aunt or uncle knows how to give shots. We could try radioing them," she suggested desperately, even though she knew that the chances of getting them were slim, due to the poor transmission from this secluded valley.

He waited, his hand out.

Sighing, she walked over, grasped the saddle horn and felt herself being lifted into the saddle by a strong grip on the back of her jeans. "Thanks," she said, trying for a touch of humor.

"Throw your leg over," he advised, leaning back in order to give her room.

She did as directed, then was straddling the horse, her legs resting against Connor's. For a moment, she didn't dare breathe as she held on with both hands, fighting the half-forgotten fear that threatened to engulf her.

The horse shook its head slightly and glanced back at her. The sound of her expelled breath was ragged, and she concentrated on drawing air into her lungs at an even rate.

"He's gentle," Connor said behind her. "A gelding, not a stallion."

"Is that better?" she managed to ask.

He chuckled. "Yes."

She felt Connor's muscles move as he tightened his legs on the gelding and urged the huge beast toward the road. His chest touched her back, and his arm brushed her side as he held the reins with his left hand. His right hand slid around her, holding her securely in his embrace.

For the first twenty minutes, she was aware only of her own feelings. Valiantly, she fought the childhood terror until, seeing that the horse did behave and Connor really did seem to be in control, she began to breathe easier.

She spent the next twenty minutes looking at the woods and the rugged trail. Relaxing even more, she let herself lean against Connor's warm strength and became lost in a daydream, just as she had when she first saw him. She shifted into a more comfortable position.

"Be still," he said.

"Wh-what?" she stuttered, startled by his order.

"Quit squirming around. The horse isn't going to hurt you."

At his reprimand, she sat up straighter, losing some of her confidence. She couldn't decide which was more dangerous: being on a horse or being in Connor's arms.

Cynthia felt Connor guide the gelding into a faster pace with the subtle urging of his thighs as they followed the rough logging road down the mountain. The trees loomed tall and silent on either side of them, like sentinels of the forests.

After a few minutes, secure in his masculine embrace, feeling protected and cherished for the first time that she could remember, she let herself relax and sink deeper and deeper into a daydream of being captured by a dashing, gallant outlaw who had taken one look at her and vowed never to let her go.

He would spirit her to his mountain hideaway, where he would claim her for his bride. The other outlaws would have a feast, with music and dancing to celebrate their boss's happiness. Then he would take her by the hand and lead her to a place apart from the others. He would lift her into his arms and carry her inside, closing the door behind them. Laying her on a bed of skins, he would say...

"Don't go to sleep."

"I won't," she replied dreamily. "Not tonight."

"I'm referring to right now. You're heavy," his voice said close to her ear, somewhat exasperated.

Cynthia bolted upright, startling the animal and Connor. The gelding pranced lightly sideways and lunged forward into a gallop. Connor held her tightly as he brought the horse under control once more.

"What's wrong with you?" he snapped, pulling tightly on the reins until they stopped at a flat place in the overgrown road.

She spoke in her most conciliating tone. "I'm sorry. I was daydreaming and didn't realize...that is, I didn't know I was leaning against you.... Is everything all right?" she ended as he slid off the saddle.

He held up his arms for her. "I'm going to let Ranger take a break before we start up the ridge."

She let herself be lifted down, and, for a second after her feet were on the ground, neither of them moved. "Is that his name?"

Connor released her and took the reins, loosely tying the gelding to a limb so he could reach some grass at the base of the tree. He nodded in answer to her question.

"He does seem gentle," she acknowledged. "Like you."

Connor's head jerked around as if he had been slapped. He glared at her. "Don't give me attributes that don't exist."

Tilting her head to one side, she studied his set expression as he unbuckled one of the saddlebags and removed its contents. He placed sandwiches on a log and motioned for her to be seated.

"I'm not. I can see for myself what you are." She picked up a thick roast beef sandwich and began eating.

Without comment, he did the same.

"It was thoughtful of you to bring something to eat. You must have realized I didn't have time for lunch today, what with flying up to Lewiston and talking to the doctor there about the treatment before coming back with the medicine. Thank you very much." She was determined to express her appreciation; she had a feeling few people in his life had been appreciative of his kind deeds.

"You're welcome."

His eyes darkened, and she wondered what they concealed. He finished his lunch and waited for her to be done.

"We'd better go. The serum..." she began, but lost the thought as he, too, moved to get up. Their lips were suddenly very close. She felt the whisper of his expelled breath across her cheek, then heard a low, wrenching groan.

His lips came toward her as he bent his head. He caught her with his arms, enclosed her, captured her. When he moved back, the heat in his gaze stole her breath away. "I've wanted to do this since the moment I saw you," he muttered, almost as if he was angry.

"Outlaw," she said softly, reaching up to caress his face. "Robin Hood of the forests."

"I'm no fictional hero," he warned.

"I know." She slipped her hand into his dark hair and closed the minute distance between them.

The kiss was all that her dreams had foretold—exciting...ravenous...scary...gentle...sweet...fulfilling....

After he eased the initial pressure, he moved his head to one side, then to the other, in order to know her lips completely. With his tongue he stroked the parted surfaces lightly before gliding inside and exploring the inner recesses for several long, breathless moments.

She returned his caress, responding with a fierce, urgent need of her own, opening herself to him and wanting him to do the same with her. She ran her fingers through his hair, loving the feel of the smooth strands against her skin. His hands were on her back, gliding from her waist to her shoulders, caressing her again and again as he might to gentle a nervous filly.

Kissing him, being kissed, was like being filled with light. She felt bright, luminous. Her heart, beating against his, raced with desire. When he drew back, she let him go.

"We'd better be on our way," he said in thickened tones.

"Yes." Her voice was husky.

Silently, they mounted, and he leaned around her and patted Ranger's neck. "Touch him," he commanded, but his tone was softer than any he had used with her before.

With fingers that trembled, she petted the horse's neck. Connor put his hand over hers, forcing her to vigorously chafe the sleek muscles.

"He likes that," he said. "Males like to be touched just as much as females." He paused. "The way you touched me."

"Did you like it?" She stopped rubbing the gelding's neck and looked over her shoulder at Connor.

"Yes." His look held her. "We have serum to deliver," he reminded her, then gave the reins a shake. Ranger started forward at a rapid clip and the land rose sharply in front of them. They still had a long way to go.

"I thought you said it would only take an hour," she reminded him after looking at her watch. It was almost four o'clock, and they were still riding.

The shadows were lengthening as the sun descended toward the peaks to the west of them. They would have a long twilight to find their way to the Graceson cabin, but she didn't like the thought of the trip back, traveling over hazardous terrain after dark.

More dangerous still was the night ahead; she would have to spend it at Connor's cabin. Her pulse leaped and her breath stuck in her throat.

"What?" he asked when she made a faint noise.

"Nothing," she replied. She clutched the saddle horn desperately as her thoughts kept churning. "It's taking a lot longer than you said."

"You were scared," he reminded her. "I didn't see any sense in adding to your fright by mentioning the long journey ahead."

"Are we nearly there?" she asked in a querulous voice.

Connor heard the weariness in her voice. She was tired, and the uneasiness between them wasn't helping any. He wished now that he hadn't kissed her. He could sense her internal struggle. Was it so terrible for her to be in his arms?

"Yes, we're almost there," he assured her. Her hair smelled of shampoo and the light scent of perfume. He suppressed the urge to bend down and bury his face against her neck; an innate sensitivity told him she wasn't ready.

Suddenly unable to stop himself, he let his lips rest briefly on the halo of soft curls that had escaped her ponytail. Like a moonstruck adolescent, he thought, mocking his growing attraction toward her.

"We're here," he said when she turned to stare at him. They rounded the bend, and the cabin was in sight a hundred yards down the road. She faced forward, her relief tangible.

"There's Mr. Graceson, coming out the door. He must have seen us."

"Saved by the bell," Connor murmured with a dry chuckle.

Cynthia let him lift her from the big gelding. "And not a moment too soon," she added on a playful note, glad that they had at last arrived.

"Thank God you're here." Mr. Graceson rushed forward, meeting them at the split-rail fence that surrounded the house. "Buddy seems to be getting worse. The swelling is increasing, I think. We just talked to the doctor. If Buddy doesn't feel any better after the serum, he said we should get him to a hospital."

Cynthia patted the distraught man's arm. "We have the medicine right here." She took the packet, once Connor had gotten it out of the saddlebag and handed it to her. "Hello, Ann," she called to a woman who came to the door and motioned for them to hurry.

Connor tied Ranger to a post and walked up the path after Cynthia and Mr. Graceson. He smiled grimly, watching as both the man and his wife treated Cynthia as if she had been sent by the gods to save their nephew. He wondered if everyone on her postal route greeted her the same way. Probably. She looked after all of them. And they thought they were independent, he silently scoffed. Not one of them realized she was the source of their independence. She was their safety net, there to rescue them when they got into trouble—like now.

He followed them into the luxurious cabin. It had been built as a fishing lodge, but had all the amenities. There was a modern kitchen with gas appliances, including a refrigerator, and a living room right out of *Better Homes and Gardens*.

The little boy, who was about six years old, was on one of the sofas. He was obviously in pain. His swollen and blotchy face was unrecognizable, his eyes mere slits in the puffy flesh. His breathing was labored.

Connor saw the alarm in Cynthia's eyes before she smiled and crossed the room.

"Hi, Buddy, I have something here to make you feel better," she said, her voice friendly. "I have to give it to you in shots, though, so it will hurt some. Would you rather take them in your arm or in your hip or one in each?''

"How many shots?'' Buddy asked in a wheezy voice.

"Two,'' she answered honestly.

"Arm,'' he requested.

She nodded and assembled the medicinal paraphernalia. In less than a minute, she had administered two shots to the boy's thin arm. He was a wiry child without much fat for padding. Connor winced as the boy withstood the shots without a whimper, although two big tears squeezed out of his eyes.

"Show me the stings, and I'll put something on them, too,'' Cynthia told Buddy, pulling out a small vial from the medicine pack. She efficiently smoothed a salve over the stings with their angry red centers, examining each one to make sure the stinger was out.

After that, Buddy seemed more comfortable and fell into a shallow sleep, his breathing loud and raspy. There was nothing more the adults could do but wait.

The other woman approached Connor. "I'm Ann Graceson.''

Connor shook hands with his hostess. "Connor O'Shaugnessy, two mountains over next to the north fork of the creek.'' He inclined his head in the direction of his house.

"I saw you ride up on a horse.'' Ann looked puzzled.

"Cynthia developed engine trouble and landed at my place. I brought her over.'' It was the first time he had said her name to someone; he liked the sound of it.

Cynthia rose from the rug by the sofa. "Did you see that monster he made me ride?'' Her teasing lifted the pall of worry, and the three adults laughed.

"Come have a cup of coffee,'' Ann invited. She led the way to the table, which was off the living room in a pass-through to the kitchen. "This is my husband, Peter. Peter, Connor lives at the old Taylor place."

The men exchanged greetings, and Peter thanked Connor for bringing Cynthia.

"It was an educational experience," Connor said easily. "I've never watched someone overcome total terror. Cynthia's frightened to death of horses."

"Not at all," she promptly denied. "It's just that I made a pact with them years ago. I'd stay off their backs if they would do the same for me."

She was inordinately pleased with Connor, as if her protégé had performed well in public. He was polite, charming and at ease, which relaxed everyone else, too. Had she expected him to act surly and impatient? Truthfully, she hadn't been at all sure how he would react to others, but there was no need to worry. He was being the perfect gentleman.

"Well, I don't care how you got here. I'm just glad you did," Ann said. "Cynthia is our Florence Nightingale," she told Connor. "She takes care of all of us."

"Remember my first emergency call? I was a wreck." Cynthia shook her head, remembering, and turned to Connor. "My first month on the job, I had to fly out an expectant mother whose baby had decided to come early. We made it to the hospital, but just barely. I decided then I'd better learn to handle all types of dire situations, so I took trauma classes—their term, not mine—at the hospital in Boise."

"I see." He looked at her and saw more than a lovely young woman; he saw a person willing to take life as it came, preparing herself as much as possible, then simply doing the best she could. He could respect a person like that.

After drinking the coffee and talking of the weather and the number of wildflowers and bees there were that year, Cynthia decided it was time to go.

"We'd better get back," she said, looking at Connor.

"Oh, you can't," Ann protested. "It's too late. You'll have to spend the night with us."

"There's plenty of room," her husband assured them. "Both the sofas pull out into beds." He glanced toward his sleeping nephew. "I guess one of you will have to take Buddy's room."

Cynthia quickly assessed the problem. Perhaps it would be better to stay here than at Connor's, where she'd be alone with him. "Connor can have the room. I'll sleep on the other sofa and keep an eye on Buddy during the night," she volunteered.

"I'll stay out here. You can have the bedroom," Connor stated in no uncertain terms.

"No, it would be better if I stayed out here," Cynthia insisted.

The Gracesons looked at each other.

"I thought I'd put Buddy in his room. He may rest more comfortably in his own bed, since he's used to sleeping there. It's right across from our room, and I'll be able to hear him if he needs me," Ann said, thus ending the brief debate. "I'll start supper now. I know you must be starved after your trip."

"I'll help." Cynthia jumped up and followed Ann into the kitchen, avoiding Connor's eyes.

"You fixing up the Taylor place for the winter?" Peter asked as the two women left the room.

She couldn't hear Connor's reply.

After Cynthia fed Buddy a few spoonfuls of soup and applied fresh salve to his stings, Connor lifted the little boy and carried him into his bedroom, where Ann had the bed turned down and ready.

Cynthia watched the way Connor handled Buddy and thought of how he would be with his own children. His touch was sure and confident, reassuring the child. His smile was kind, his gaze gentle. He would be a good father, she thought. He would set a good example for his children. When Connor straightened up, she left the room quickly, blinking her eyes rapidly to remove the trace of tears. He followed her out.

Connor and Cynthia talked to the Gracesons for a long time before they ambled off to bed. The women checked Buddy and decided he was somewhat better, his breathing easier.

The short sofa that Buddy had earlier occupied had been pulled out into a bed for her, Cynthia saw on her return to the living room. Covers had been placed on the longer sofa for Connor. The sound of a shower indicated he was in the bathroom.

Flipping through a magazine, she waited until he finished so she could wash up. A quick shower was just what she needed, too.

When Connor reappeared, she wasn't prepared for his masculine presence or the sheer force of his blatant maleness. He wore his jeans and a white T-shirt. His chest looked inviting, broad and strong. His arms would be welcoming—she was sure of that when she met his eyes. He grinned at her.

Her heart stopped, then raced like mad. He had the most engaging grin—mischievous and fun-loving, but with a certain innocence reserved only for the very young, as though he still expected Santa Claus to come down the chimney and bring him all his heart's desires. She was suddenly afraid for him, afraid that he would never know the happiness of loving and being loved equally in return. It was an odd thought, she chided herself, ridiculous, really.

She watched as he walked over to his bed. His hands paused at the fastening of his jeans, and he looked at her with raised brows and an amused expression. Turning away, she rose abruptly and went to the bathroom.

Cynthia's heartbeat didn't slow until she was halfway through her shower. Her imagination kept painting pictures of a lean, sinewy torso and narrow hips and powerful arms.... He was under the covers when she returned.

The living room was dark except for the glow from the fireplace. Connor had built up the fire again, she noted. She wore a flannel nightgown lent to her by Ann. A pair of blue pajamas had been laid out in the bathroom, but Connor had elected not to wear them. She was intensely aware of that fact.

After lying down, she gazed at the fire, knowing that Connor was doing the same. Fatigue settled like lead in her every limb, but she couldn't go to sleep. Closing her eyes determinedly, she tried singing songs to herself, but her mind kept playing slow love songs, intensifying her restlessness.

She stared into the flames again and sighed discontentedly, wondering how she was going to endure this night. Her amber gaze flicked across the room as she heard Connor stir. To her amazement, he came to her. She didn't know if she would protest or fall into his arms; she was still wondering when he stopped beside her.

"Turn over," he ordered gruffly.

She stared up at him, her mind refusing to understand his intention. His body was outlined against the glow of the fire, which turned his flesh to bronze, his T-shirt and white briefs to gold.

"I'll give you a massage. You're probably sore from riding. Turn over on your stomach."

She did and immediately felt his weight beside her and his hands on her shoulders. He rubbed her neck, pressing the tender spots with pinpoint precision. Gradually he moved down her back, and the tension slowly evaporated from her slender body. She yawned widely and snuggled deeper into the pillow.

"I'm sleepy now. You can quit," she said. "Thank you very much," she added politely.

"You're welcome." Laughter rippled through his deep voice, and he kept on with his task. He pushed the covers farther down and massaged her buttocks, knowing those would be the tenderest of all from the unaccustomed ride.

A small groan escaped her as he probed deeply into sore muscles, then she sighed with pleasure as his touch stroked away the accumulated aches of the day. He smiled a bit, finding a kind of peace in his chore.

As the exhaustion was rubbed out of her body, Cynthia became more alert, even though she was half asleep. The cares of the day and her worries over Buddy faded. Slowly, she became attuned to her body.

The warmth of Connor's massaging fingers permeated her entire being. She felt cozy, relaxed, yet gradually awakened to the allure of physical fulfillment. When his strokes glided into caresses, she turned over and faced him.

His hands continued their slow, sensuous movements, moving over her shoulders and down her arms, all the way to her wrists. He lifted one hand and caressed each finger, then he did the same to the other.

Lacing his fingers through hers, palm to palm, he brought her hand to his mouth and sensuously trailed kisses over the back of it. His eyes blazed into hers.

"Who are you," he asked hoarsely, "that you can make me forget everything I've learned these past few months? "You've invaded my life, ruined my peace of mind, and now you torture me with the promise of paradise."

His eyes appeared haunted, and she reached up to smooth away the frown lines. He caught her hand before she could touch him.

"What do you want from me?" he demanded.

She answered without considering. "Everything, I think."

His face hardened. "There's only this." His lips took hers with savage tenderness, not deepening the kiss, just holding at the edge of total bliss.

Responding to the hunger that seemed to come from her soul, she wrapped both arms around him and pulled him down to her. With a low groan, he stretched out beside her, his large body covering hers. She felt his desire grow and harden.

"Not here. We can't make love here," she whispered, reminding him of their vulnerable location.

"I know," he murmured, kissing her ear and the side of her neck. "If we had gone back to my place..."

He didn't need to complete the statement. They both longed for the privacy of his cabin. Cynthia had never before become this lost in the physical love of a relationship. It was new and startling and irresistibly exciting.

With trembling fingers, she slipped her hands under his T-shirt and touched the smooth flesh of his back, exploring each muscle and the outline of his spine. He felt so incredibly good to her. When his mouth came back to hers, she clutched his shoulders, desperately holding on to the one steady thing in a world that was spinning slowly out of control.

When his hand caressed along her side, then glided upward to cup her breast, she held her breath as he rubbed her nipple, bringing it into bas-relief against the flannel. Then she released a ragged sigh. He smiled against her mouth.

He did exactly what he knew would bring her to the brink of madness, then he would let her slide back a bit before renewing his assault. His mouth, his hands, every part of him, knew how to draw a response from every part of her.

Her gown had four buttons down the front, and he unfastened them one at a time, then frowned. "How does it come off?"

"Over my head."

"Damn," he exclaimed softly, grinning mischievously. "It's better that way. If I got you naked, I probably wouldn't be able to stop."

"Me either," she agreed, gasping slightly as he closed his mouth over her straining breast.

Connor chuckled at her obvious agitation, then became serious as he tasted the wonder of her. Her breast was small, with a pert nipple that was tannish pink and came to a blunt point at the tip. He ran his tongue around it until she squirmed beneath him, giving him a taste of what it would feel like to have the rest of her body joined to his. He wanted her with a raging passion unlike any he could recall experiencing.

The discipline of thirty-two years fought and won the battle over whether he should make love to her right then and there. She was right; this was not the time. Later, he thought, there would be another time. . . .

"I want to sleep with you in my arms all night," he told her, lifting his mouth from the feast of her breasts.

She knew her eyes were dreamy and revealing, but at that moment it didn't seem to matter: she had nothing to conceal from this man.

She pulled up his T-shirt and splayed her fingers through the mat of hair covering his chest. Her skin seemed pale and ethereal next to his deep tan. He was like the trees in the forest—solid and substantial.

She thought of him as a bulwark against the wounds of life, a safe place she could crawl into and be warm and happy. Cherished—yes, that was the word.

"Cherished," she murmured.

"What?" He kissed the corner of her mouth, his tongue tracing her lips.

"You make me feel safe—cherished. It's the nicest feeling," she explained. Her vision was hazy as she gazed up at him. Carefully, she smoothed back a wave of fiery hair over his forehead. "It looks as if it would burn me when I touch you. But it doesn't. It only sets me on fire." She laughed softly at her own musing.

"If you knew what I'm feeling, you might not feel so safe," he warned, his eyes dark with male desire.

Remembering that he was the one who had been recently wounded, she slid her arms around him and pressed her cheek to his chest. "You're safe with me," she assured him.

He greeted her outrageous remark with silent laughter. "I think I'm about to come apart. That's how safe I am with you," he teased, his tone light.

With renewed energy, he descended upon her mouth with devastating kisses that left her weak and hungry for more. She briefly wondered what he would be like as a lover if he truly loved someone. And how it would feel to be that person.

His lips were greedy on her flesh, rushing over her face, her neck and breasts. With careful hands, he touched each burgeoning mound until she was fully peaked into tempting rosebuds of delight. He chuckled, obviously liking the effect of his ministrations. Then he sucked gently, as if taking nourishment from her. She became filled with a passionate tenderness that was wild and beautiful at the same time.

"Cyn."

The sound of her name spoken passionately was almost her undoing. She clung to him shamelessly, wanting him with a demanding hunger that consumed them both. When he at last drew back, she felt totally exposed in her need. He kissed her eyes closed.

"Sleep," he advised, his voice deep, quiet. "Tomorrow will be here before we know it."

He turned her over and began rubbing her back, each stroke designed to damp the fires of passion he had built in her. She wondered if he knew how much power he had over her. At that moment, she would have done anything he requested. She let herself sink into dreams of them alone together.

He continued to caress her spine long after she was asleep. When the fire died down and the room turned cool, he covered her, tucking the quilts and blankets in around her shoulders and went to his bed. He lay there and listened to the wind for a long time before he slept.

Cynthia roused briefly from her slumber at four the next morning. Connor was building up the fire to drive off the chill in the early-morning air before everyone else woke up.

Remembering his massage, she was sure that in spite of the sexual tension that had sprung up between them, he was a considerate person. His main intent had not been to seduce but to soothe her aching body. The passion had grown of its own accord. A man like that just couldn't be wasted; the world needed him too much.

She fastened a tender smile on her lips as she observed his silhouette against the rising flames. There was one other thing she was sure of: he didn't think of her as a sister.

Four

When the room was comfortably warm, Cynthia rose and went to the bathroom to dress. She met Ann in the doorway to Buddy's room on her return, and together they went in to check on him.

"The swelling is down, don't you think?" Ann asked anxiously, leaning over the sleeping child.

Cynthia thought he had definitely improved.

Buddy stirred and opened his eyes. "Aunt Ann, I want to go home," he requested in a wobbly tone.

"Of course, darling," she crooned, placing a hand on his forehead and checking his temperature. "How do you feel?"

"Okay, I guess. Itchy."

Ann looked at Cynthia. "I'd feel better if he were closer to help if he needs it. Could you take him back to Boise with you? We have the Blazer, but one section of the logging road is still washed out from the last storm, according to the ranger we talked to yesterday on the radio. That's why we had to ask you to fly the serum in. Buddy's father is anxious to have him home. Do you think your plane will be working soon?''

''I'm sure the problem is in the fuel line, and it shouldn't take long to clear it. Let's talk to Connor,'' Cynthia suggested.

He was in the kitchen, pouring a cup of fresh-perked coffee. He looked domesticated, but retained an air of danger—like a tame bear, she thought.

''Buddy wants to go home,'' she said, understanding the child's need to be with his parents. ''Do you think we can get him over to your place and fly him out?''

He laid a hand on her shoulder as if he would soothe her emotions the way he had soothed her tired body. ''If we fix the plane, you can fly over and pick him up. Can you ride Ranger alone? I'll be right beside you, but I'll have to walk on the uphill sections. The weight on the horse would be too much for the whole trip.''

Cynthia looked startled, then resigned. Her smile was wan. ''I suppose so. The postmaster didn't say anything about riding horses, but he would probably expect it along with the rain, snow, sleet and gloom of night.''

''Right.'' He ruffled her hair and turned back to take a deep swallow of the black coffee.

Within an hour they were ready to leave. Cynthia sat in the saddle. Connor, reins gathered in his capable hand, led the way. On relatively level terrain, he jogged, keeping Ranger clipping along at a fast pace. When they started up the steep ridge, horse and man both slowed, breathing heavily as they climbed the gully-slashed trail.

The old logging road rose in a series of hairpin turns, twelve switchbacks in all, before reaching the peak of the hill. Connor paused to regain his breath.

"Here, you ride and let me walk," Cynthia offered. He looked exhausted.

Connor shook his head and started downhill. It made him feel funny inside to have someone be concerned about him. Only Sister Barnabas had worried about his health as he took one odd job after another after school in order to earn money. Only Barney had cared if he was tired. And now this woman.

Cynthia thought her bones were going to poke through her backside with each step the gelding took. They finally entered the stretch of road crossing the narrow valley to Connor's cabin. Once out of the woods, she noticed the wind kicking up and the gathering of black clouds on the mountain peaks.

A storm. Just what they needed, she thought glumly. Wasn't anything going to go right this trip? She was now two days behind on her mail delivery. A simple mission of mercy had somehow become a complicated situation.

"I'll have to get the fuel line cleared and take off. There's a storm building," she said, eyeing the rapidly darkening sky.

"Right." He stopped and climbed into the saddle behind her. Wrapping his strong arms around her, he urged the horse into a rocking canter that was much easier than the jarring trot.

In another twenty minutes they arrived back at Connor's place without mishap. "See about your plane," Connor advised. "I'll take care of Ranger."

She ran down to the aircraft. In a few minutes he joined her, and together they checked out the gas line. Finally, over an hour later, they found the problem—debris trapped in a bend in the linkage. Connor ran a piece of wire through the line and unplugged it, and then they put everything back together. Cynthia tried the starter. The engine coughed once, then purred smoothly, and all the gauges indicated the plane was ready to go.

"I'll see you tomorrow?" he asked.

Glancing worriedly at the approaching storm, she shook her head. "Probably Friday. I have mail to deliver." She smiled, motioned for the painter to be untied and taxied out into the quiet waters of the cove. The plane lifted easily, and she turned it toward the Graceson place. In another thirty minutes she was taking off again, this time bound for Boise and home for her small passenger. She picked up the mike, relayed the message that she was on her way and was told Buddy's father would meet them at the airport with an ambulance.

Cynthia looked at the sky as she paused outside the hospital. The storm had dogged her flight, and now the sky was a depressing gray. It was probably raining in the mountains. She thought of Connor and wondered what he was doing at this moment. Was he angry with her for involving him in the emergency? She shrugged; it couldn't be helped.

Now that Buddy was in safe hands, she felt light-headed with relief. The doctors had assured her and Buddy's father that the boy was in no immediate danger, but they would keep him in the hospital overnight for observation.

She wished she could get word to Connor and to Buddy's aunt and uncle so they wouldn't worry. Tomorrow she would try to contact the Gracesons on their CB radio, and she would leave a message at the ranger station and the general store, located on the county road where the logging road ended, to let everyone else know the child was going to be okay.

There was no way she could get hold of Connor. He would just have to wait until she was over his way again.

If the storm lasted very long, that could be days. Restless, she decided to visit Mr. Taylor and see how he was getting along.

At the senior citizens home, she found the old man in the lounge, playing cards. He looked good, better than he had in ages. "What's the secret of your youth?" she wanted to know, kissing his leathery cheek.

"I'm winning," he explained, indicating his bridge hand. He introduced her to his companions, a widow and a married couple who had decided to give up their house and take life easy. "Cindy Lou was my postman," he told his friends, using his pet name shortened from Cynthia Louise.

After the game, Cynthia and Mr. Taylor went into the sun room and watched the storm lash the windows.

"Did you notice the widow?" Mr. Taylor asked. At her nod, he continued, "I've got designs on her."

Cynthia laughed with delight. "Does she know?"

"If she doesn't, she will soon," he declared, giving her a big grin. "How's the homestead?"

She told him about the emergency with Buddy. "Did you meet Connor O'Shaugnessy when you sold the house to him?" she asked when she had finished her story.

"Sure did. Had him come up and stay a few days to be sure he knew what he was getting into. My son tends to make things sound better than they actually are. Is O'Shaugnessy settled in? He had a lot of plans to fix up the place."

"It's looking very nice. New shingles and windows. I've only peeked at the inside, but I think he's done a lot there, too."

"Good. It needed new blood to breathe some life back into it. A place gets old and run-down, just like a person."

"You don't look old and run-down," she protested.

He smiled broadly, showing off a new set of teeth. "I have to admit, this place has given me a new lease on life. I was drying up out there by myself. After my wife died, I didn't want to be around anyone, but now, well, it's all right."

Cynthia curled her legs under her and rested against the arm of the easy chair. "Do you think it's good for someone to be alone after they've been hurt?"

His glance was shrewd. "If you mean O'Shaugnessy, I don't know. Sometimes a man needs to be alone in order to find himself again. Maybe he needs to establish contact with his own values, with how he sees himself as a man. He took a pretty hard beating during the trial. The newspapers were up in arms in righteous indignation at his abusing the opportunities he had been given. Seems to me he earned everything he got; nothing was given to him."

She nodded slowly, thinking of his lonely years in the orphanage. He had earned scholarships to go to school and had worked on road construction jobs to buy his food and clothing.

"I don't think it's good for him to be by himself," she said. "He's not bitter, not yet, but loneliness could twist his whole life. You should have seen him with Buddy. He was wonderful."

"And you've decided to save him from himself," Mr. Taylor concluded with a twinkle in his eyes.

She frowned. "Adam doesn't want me to get involved. He says I'm too gullible about my lame ducks—" She stopped, but it was too late.

Mr. Taylor laughed aloud at her embarrassment. "This is one duck you can stop worrying about."

"I can see that." She wrinkled her nose at him and gave him a teasing grimace. "I'd better warn the widow."

"You'll do no such thing. I've practically got her eating out of my hand." He sobered. "Well, young Cindy, I just don't know what to tell you about your injured friend. Just don't let a good man go to waste."

"He needs something to bring him out of his shell—maybe a new job—before he loses his self-worth." She brightened. "That's it! He needs someone to offer him a new position, one of responsibility, to show confidence in him." Her mouth drooped. "I don't know anyone in construction."

"Why, sure you do."

"Who?"

"John Graceson."

"Buddy's father?" She pictured the worried man who had met her plane and whisked his son off to the hospital.

"Sure. He's head of the largest road construction firm in the state. Didn't you know that?"

"No. Peter and Ann didn't mention it."

"Graceson is a power in this state. If he put O'Shaugnessy in charge, no one would doubt his judgment."

She thought it over. "Do you think it would be terribly pushy of me to mention Connor to him?"

"Wouldn't hurt," the old man assured her. "Of course, your young man might be inclined to disagree."

She considered the consequences. Connor had a lot of pride, and a lot of anger. His faith in people had been badly shaken. He needed someone to show faith in him. Yes, she decided, she would talk to Mr. Graceson. Connor might be furious, but it was for his own good. Tonight, when she went to the hospital to visit Buddy, if the boy's father was there, she would speak to him and ask his advice about Connor. She smiled and took a deep breath.

* * *

A tiny smile still flitted around Cynthia's mouth as she banked into the turn. Her heart beat faster as the calm surface of the small lagoon rose to meet the pontoons on the plane. It was Tuesday, almost a week since she had last landed there. Then, Connor had come running to her, having heard the engine quit.

Would he come to her today?

After killing the motor and tying up, she stood on the pier and looked up the meandering path to the house. He stood on the front porch but made no move toward her.

She pulled a large sack from the plane. "Lunch," she called. "My treat."

He walked across the meadow.

"Do you like fried chicken?" She was afraid of his silence. He had retreated into his shell, once again the wary bear who disliked humans.

"Is there any mail?" he asked.

"No. I'm here for a picnic." Her amber eyes defied him to order her away.

He sighed heavily. "Yes, I like chicken." He took a seat on the opposite end of the dock, leaning against the corner post. He didn't look at her.

She felt somewhat daunted by his unfriendly attitude. After what had happened between them, she had expected a warmer welcome.

"Did you make it through that terrible storm last Wednesday with no damage? When I talked to Ann and Peter the next day, they said more of the road had washed out. I was worried about—"

"I had no problems," he cut her off.

"Good."

She carried a box of fried chicken, rolls, finger vegetables and corn on the cob to him. He accepted it with a muttered "Thanks" that didn't sound very grateful.

"You're welcome," she said dryly, wanting to give him a hard shake. She sat down at her favorite place and began eating. The quiet was penetrating, and she relaxed in the peace of the homestead.

"How's Buddy?" he finally asked.

"Doing great," she replied enthusiastically. "He went home on Friday and was out riding his bike when I stopped by Sunday."

Connor smiled, and she breathed easier.

"Did you know Buddy's father is John Graceson, head of Tristate Asphalt Corporation?"

The smile disappeared from his face. "No," he said slowly. Wariness masked his eyes. "What about him?"

Now she knew this wasn't the right time, but she had already started. "When I told him how you had helped get the serum to his son, he recognized your name."

Connor gave her a level glance. "Is that right?"

After swallowing a suddenly dry piece of chicken, she continued. "He's interested in you. There's a job his company has bid on for the state, a big one, and he wants the best..."

Her voice trailed off at Connor's strange smile. There was no gentleness or humor or friendliness in it.

"Does he?" he inquired sardonically.

"Yes," she answered, knowing she had overstepped his boundaries. Obviously Buddy's emergency hadn't shown him anything about people needing people. He'd only made the best of a forced situation. She was disappointed.

They finished the picnic lunch without speaking. When she stuffed her refuse back in the bag, he stood and did the same.

"Well, I guess I'd better be going," she said. She didn't like the gleam in his eye.

"Not so fast." He tossed the sack up on the bank next to the path. "We have something we didn't finish the other night. Remember?" His voice dropped to sexy depths that caused a shiver to run down her spine.

He took her in his arms.

"What are you doing?" she asked, her voice trembling slightly. She certainly wasn't afraid of him; he wouldn't hurt her, even if he was angry.

His answer was in his kiss. It started out in fury, his mouth hard and demanding on hers, but as it progressed, it gentled until it was as sweet as any they had shared on Wednesday night. She yielded to it.

Molding herself against him, she let the embrace carry her like a thistle seed on the wind, lifting her higher and higher, spinning her around and around as if she were attached to a thread of silk.

"Ummm," she murmured, happy once more. Her arms enclosed him, and she gave in to the kiss, letting the heady potion of mutual attraction bind them to each other.

Cynthia thought that as long as she could reach the core of kindness in him, she had a chance to save him from the abyss of bitterness that threatened him. If she could reach him this way, through their kiss, then she would eventually reach him in other ways, too, through the heart and the mind.

He lifted her in his strong arms—his muscles were as hard as a tree trunk—and carried her to the grassy slope of the meadow. Bees hummed around them, but neither noticed as they reclined among the wildflowers.

He moved his mouth hungrily over her face. She turned so that their lips met. The kiss was deeply satisfying to her, and she was filled with wonder at how easy it was to accept the idea of a physical union with this man when she hadn't with another.

He taught her things about her own nature she hadn't realized. If she returned him to the world, whole and well, the world would be the better for it, and so would she. Smiling against the embrace of their lips, she wondered whether her reasoning was wise or foolish.

As if sensing her thoughts, he lifted his head. She gazed into the fathomless pools of his eyes, spellbound by the richness of life she detected in those verdant depths.

"Don't move," she advised, fear darkening her amber eyes.

"What?" He frowned down at her.

"There's a bee on your hair, right above your forehead," she whispered, afraid of disturbing the small, dangerous creature.

"I'm not allergic to bee venom," he said, giving his head a shake. The bee flew off.

Cynthia reached up and smoothed the lock of hair off his face. "So tough," she said, feeling incredibly tender toward him. She caressed his hand between her shoulder and her cheek. "So gentle. And lonely. I'll send my brother to you. You both need a friend."

He pulled away. Sitting with his arms propped on his drawn-up knees, he stared off into the distance. "I don't need your help, neither in my personal life nor my career." He looked as if he were carved of stone.

"Yes, but—"

He turned to her. "You don't have to send anyone to me. I can find my own friends. The same goes for a job. I can find that, too. If I had wanted to talk to Graceson, I would have done it without any interference from you. I don't need a do-gooder like you directing my life.''

''Yes, you do,'' she insisted, sitting up and glaring at him. Their faces were no more than six inches apart. ''You're hibernating here in the wilds, instead of facing the world. You need to get back to work.''

''I'll decide what I need and when I need it. Dammit, stay out of my life.''

He looked so frustrated, so aggravated, that she had to forcibly suppress her rising sense of humor. Now she spoke softly, with gently reprimanding logic. ''You need someone to restore your faith in people.'' She propped her elbow on her knee and her chin in her hand, glancing at him with a mocking grin. She was sure of her ground. The fact that he was fighting her proved she was hitting close to the truth.

''Take care of your brother,'' he advised, coolly cynical. ''What's he doing out here in the mountains, digging around in old mines? Why don't you try to get him back into the mainstream?''

''That was his problem. He needed to get out of it and find a new life for himself. Right now he's truly interested in mining. Later he may become involved in something else, but it will be his decision.''

''My decision is to stay here for a while...alone.'' He took a deep breath and slowly released it as his gaze swept the meadow. ''I thought there'd be no one to bother me here,'' he added succinctly.

''You see,'' she announced triumphantly, ''you're withdrawing. You use this as a place to shun people. That's not making a new life for yourself. I've seen your work. You belong in construction. You're a natural builder.''

She didn't tell him those were the very words Mr. Graceson had used to her when she had told him about

Connor. "The man's a genius," he had exclaimed. "I've seen his work. He has an innate understanding of materials and how to use them, as well as the training and experience. A man like that would never put out an inferior product."

His words had greatly bolstered her faith in Connor's ability. Having it confirmed by someone who knew the business made her more determined to help him.

"What do you know about it?" he demanded heatedly, his temper rising at her insistence.

"Nothing," she admitted calmly. "Mr. Graceson told me you were the best. I believed him."

His eyes, as hard as malachite, flashed. "So, you believed him, did you?" he asked softly, dangerously. "What else do you believe? That you will lure me back to civilization with the promise of your smile?" He flicked his gaze down her slender body. "Do you see yourself as my mentor, guiding me along the path you've so wisely chosen?"

Suddenly she was on her back and he was looming over her, holding down her hands at either side of her head, his large body sprawling over hers, his legs holding hers captive. She returned his gaze boldly but said nothing.

"Your eyes look so clear, so innocent. Are you innocent, Cyn?" He drawled her name, taunting her. "Can any woman truly have the honesty that shines in your eyes?"

She turned her head and kissed the back of his hand, startling him. He jerked away from her as if she had bitten him. "I am a virgin, if that's what you're asking," she told him, sitting up again and watching him as he strode onto the pier, pacing its length like a caged beast.

"Why?" he asked suddenly. "You're a passionate woman. Beautiful and desirable. A lot of men must have wanted you."

"Well, most of the men I've known seemed to think of me as their kid sister," she explained. "I never fell madly in love with anyone, and no one ever fell madly in love with me—except Wyatt. He was ten and had too many teeth and his ears stuck out. I was nine and thought he was disgusting. He was always trying to kiss me. It was awful."

Connor sat on one of the corner posts. "You seem to have changed your mind about kissing," he remarked, cool and controlled once again.

"Only about the kisser and the kissee," she said, laughing merrily. Her glance from beneath her long lashes invited his kisses.

"I'm not getting involved with you, or any woman," he said firmly. "I came here to think about where I want to go in my life... without interruption."

Meeting his blank gaze, she saw that he was shielding himself from any relationship at all. Only if he admitted he wanted her, that he needed someone, would she be able to break through to him.

She rose, made her way to the plane and untied the ropes, tossing them inside. "Hang out a handkerchief if you need me," she said, climbing into the plane. In a few minutes, she took off. Looking down, she saw that he still stood where she had left him, alone on the dock.

A stubborn light gleamed in her eyes. She wasn't giving up, not by any means. This was merely a strategic retreat.

Five

The storms started the last week in June. Cynthia was delayed in making her rounds due to the weather's severity. Although she was willing to deliver mail in the rain, snow and gloom of night, the plane couldn't take it, so she was grounded for eight days of the first two weeks of July.

She hadn't been back to Connor's place, neither to deliver mail nor to have a picnic. She had decided to give him the solitude he had requested. In his present mood, he certainly wasn't receptive to any of her bright ideas.

Glancing at the clouds on the horizon, she forced her wandering mind to concentrate on the task at hand. She had a lot of mail to deliver before another storm caught up with her.

She flew over the hills and started back to Boise late in the afternoon. Her patrons had been so delighted to see her after the intermittent service that they had delayed her departures again and again, asking her a thousand questions and inviting her in for meals. Even though she had politely declined the invitations, she had been unable to stick to her tight schedule. Now she wouldn't be able to outrun the storm.

She had stopped by her brother's early that morning and found him deep in the mine, having broken through into another tunnel.

"This may be the one where Uncle Abbot found his gold," he had told her, excited about his find.

She shook her head. As long as he was happy, she wasn't going to complain, but she didn't like digging around in the dirt the way Adam did. "You should have been a gopher," she had teased him when he took a coffee break. No doubt he was back digging by now, she thought, heading toward his place. He wouldn't even know there was a storm until he came out, late in the day.

As she followed the path of the river valley, she knew she wasn't going to put down at Adam's cabin. There was only one place she wanted to go to wait out the storm. She let an updraft lift her over the ridge and into the steep valley of the north fork of French Creek.

She was almost at the lagoon when the head winds caught up with her. The wings of the small plane seesawed back and forth as she fought the storm. With a crosswind, she wasn't going to be able to make her usual approach. She turned and tried again.

If she flew directly into the wind, she would have to put the plane into a steep drop in order to land on the water. Wind shear would be the biggest danger, possibly causing her to nosedive or flip. Since water was easier to crash into than land, she waited for the gusts to die down.

Using all her skill, she landed the craft safely and bumped gently against the pier. She jumped out and lashed it to the pilings, then ran for the cabin just as the rain started.

Connor opened the door before she could knock. "Well, if it isn't the flying postlady," he drawled.

Ignoring his remark, she stepped past him. "I'm wet," she complained, standing just inside the door and grinning up at him.

He handed her a towel.

So he must have been watching, she speculated as she wiped the raindrops off her face and arms. Glancing at him, she realized he looked rather unkempt. What had he been doing?

His hair was long and rather shaggy, and he had allowed his beard to grow. It was a shade darker than his hair and very curly. It looked striking with his dark eyebrows. His eyes seemed darker than she remembered, dark and angry.

"Don't you know better than to be out in a small plane in this weather?" he demanded.

She suddenly realized he had been worried about her, and resisted an urge to step forward into his arms. She knew that with Connor, it was better to keep things light. "Let me see if I have the correct place," she murmured, pretending to read the address on an imaginary letter. "Hmm, to the Grouch Who Lives on the North Fork of French Creek. Yes," she decided, looking at Connor, "this must be it."

She managed to maintain a straight face as he glowered at her. "Where the hell have you been for the past month?" he wanted to know, a definite complaint in his tone.

"Leaving you alone. That's what you said you wanted. The postmaster doesn't like us to harass our postal patrons. Makes for bad public relations."

"So what are you doing here now?" He slipped his hands into his back pockets and gave her a challenging glance.

"I had to take shelter from the storm. Your place was close by." She walked over to the fireplace. "A fire would be nice." She couldn't look at him, afraid she would burst out laughing. He obviously didn't know whether to be glad or mad to see her.

He came to her and lifted her chin, forcing her to meet his gaze. "Your brother lives just over the next hill."

"Yes." His nearness after weeks of not seeing him was doing strange things to her vital functions. Her pulse had increased alarmingly, and her breathing was shallow. A shiver rushed through her.

He glowered at the goose bumps on her arms. "You're cold," he said, releasing her and stepping toward the woodbox. In a few minutes, he had a blazing fire going, which helped drive the chill from the room.

He stalked into the bedroom, and she used the time to have a good look around. A bearskin rug covered the varnished pine floor before the hearth. Hadn't she dreamed about lying with him on a rug in front of the fire?

"Here. I don't have a robe, but this shirt will cover most of you, if you want to get out of those damp clothes." He tossed a flannel shirt to her from the doorway and turned toward the kitchen. "Supper will be ready in thirty minutes," he called over his shoulder.

She pulled the shirt on over her blouse and slacks. She wasn't so wet that she couldn't dry her clothes with body heat. Besides, she didn't trust the precarious emotions that existed between her and Connor.

She settled down in a corner of the sofa, kicked her shoes off and pulled her feet under her. She noticed that the couch was the same one Mr. Taylor had had, but a new cover had been stretched over it. The easy chair had also been covered. A couple of tables, a rocker and a straight chair were the only other pieces of furniture in the cozy room.

"Can I help?" she called out, smelling delicious odors coming from the kitchen.

"No," he said gruffly, though not harshly. He seemed to be undergoing a mood change, his anger inexplicably gone.

"Which perhaps proves the maxim," she said with a wise nod of her head.

"What?" He came to the door. His beard was gone, and his hair, while still long, had been dampened and neatly combed back from his face. He looked less intimidating.

"I was reminding myself that to calm the raging beast, you have to feed him."

His grin was sardonic. "I thought you said you were a terrible cook."

"Yes, well, I'd have to use frozen dinners or send out to Mountainman's Pizza," she quipped. "Is dinner ready? I'm starved. Whatever you're cooking smells wonderful."

He lifted his dark brows. "Nice to know I'm appreciated for something. I was beginning to think you didn't care."

"I've checked on you every Tuesday and Friday that I made my rounds," she informed him, the conversation taking on a deeper meaning. "You didn't have a handkerchief out, and I had no mail for you."

She paused to wait for his response. Was he going to tell her that he had missed her? That he wanted her?

"Dinner." He inclined his head toward the table and crossed the room to pour the coffee.

Hiding a slight feeling of disappointment, she took her place and waited for him. The meal was simple—a pot roast with potatoes, onions and carrots. Cornbread squares were on a plate in the middle of the oak table alongside a tub of margarine.

"You're from the South, aren't you?" she asked, then picked up a square, sliced it open and generously buttered it.

"I was born in Virginia, but my father moved west when I was five." His expression was withdrawn.

"Was that before or after your mother died?" she asked, tilting her head to study his reaction.

A muscle worked in the side of his jaw. "After."

"And your father died when you were nine?"

"He left me at the orphanage. Would you like the whole story of my life?" he inquired with mendacious sincerity.

"Yes." She smiled, undaunted by his sweeping glare. "You asked," she reminded him.

He sighed, picked up his fork and began eating. Gradually his stern features relaxed. When she looked up to tell him the food was delicious, her breath caught at the brooding hunger in his eyes, and she didn't know whether to be pleased or frightened. His passion, once unleashed, might prove more than she could handle in her limited experience.

"How did you learn to cook?" she questioned, her interest in his past unfeigned.

"At the orphanage, there was a nun, Sister Barnabas— we called her Barney when the other nuns weren't around. She thought everyone should be able to cook and clean. She taught me."

Cynthia heard the unconscious affection in his voice. So he had once loved someone who hadn't betrayed or deserted him. That was good, she thought. "She must have been nice."

"She was."

She imagined him as a boy, stoic and independent. She was glad he'd had Sister Barnabas to love. It didn't seem as if life at the orphanage had been terribly bad, but it wasn't the same as a home.

"Did you ever hear from your father?"

His face became withdrawn. "He got a job in a logging camp. He wrote every Christmas, usually sent a few dollars. During my last year in high school, he caught the flu and died."

"I'm sorry."

He didn't refute her sympathy but merely looked at her for a long minute as if trying to fathom her motives.

"How did you happen to learn to fly?" He finally broke the silence, startling her out of her contemplation.

She disliked telling him; her life seemed ostentatious compared with his. "When I was sixteen, my father asked what I wanted for my birthday. I told him flying lessons, so that's what I got."

"Your folks must have money."

"They do. I don't." She wanted to make it clear she stood on her own two feet.

"How did you get to be a postlady?"

"Well, when I got out of college, I discovered no one wanted to hire a humanities major. For a year, I did odd jobs for a secretarial service. About that time, I decided Adam needed to get out of town. A friend told me about this job, I passed the exam, submitted my bid and here I am."

Connor knew her simple compression of details was far from the whole truth. "Do you support your brother?"

"We have a partnership."

Her expression warned him not to criticize her relationship with Adam. The man who took her would get the brother, too, he thought for no apparent reason. He certainly didn't intend to take on this paragon. She was so virtuous, she'd drive a man crazy in no time.

Not that he was going to make the attempt, he reminded himself coolly.

"You ought to stick to your brother," he advised. "You can get into trouble, barging into a man's home."

Her temper flared at his condescending tone. "Thank you, Father O'Shaugnessy. Any other lessons on life you think I need?" She took a bite of roast and chewed vigorously.

"Several," he snapped, "but I'm not going to be the one to give them to you."

"Good."

They ate in seething silence for several minutes before Cynthia put her fork down and sipped on her coffee. She stole a glance at Connor. He was so angry with her that he looked as though he were about to explode any minute. She grinned. "I think this is the strangest quarrel I've ever had," she remarked, watching him fill his plate again. He could easily eat twice as much as she.

"Who's quarreling?" He cocked one arrogant brow at her in a superior male gesture.

She lifted hers just as loftily. When he grimaced, she smiled.

"I realize the secret of your success," he remarked. "You get your way by driving people to the brink of madness."

She shrugged. "Whatever it takes..." She let the thought trail off into silence.

He wondered if she knew how good she looked, sitting across the table from him. Her hair was in its usual disorder of corkscrew curls around her face. His shirt hung loosely over her clothing, reminding him of how small she was and of how feminine she had felt to him when she had lain beneath his body.

When he finished his stew, she stood and collected the dishes. Without asking, she found the dishpan and soap and began washing up. He drank his coffee and watched her.

A man could get used to having a woman around, he cautioned himself. A woman had the ability to insinuate herself into a man's life until he was trapped before he knew what had happened.

He thought of the past six weeks. He had seen her only a few times, had held her and kissed her—three times at the very most—and then had been desperately lonely when she had taken him at his word and not returned for a month.

He looked away from her enticing figure. She was just a woman, like any other; she made him feel nothing that a quick toss in the hay wouldn't cure. He wanted her; that was all this agitation was. She stirred him up. Irritably, he pushed a strand of hair out of his eyes.

"Would you like your hair cut?" she asked, hanging up the drying towel.

"What? Uh, no, that's all right." He pushed the lock off his forehead again.

"I'm pretty good. I've been doing Adam's for two years."

If her brother let her do his hair, she probably wouldn't make too much of a mess of it. And his hair did need cutting. He had let himself go during the past month. Rubbing his smooth chin, he admitted that a haircut wouldn't hurt.

"I guess you can try it," he told her.

"Do you have a scissors and towel?"

In a few minutes, she had moved him to the middle of the kitchen floor, the towel fastened around his neck. She expertly combed his hair and lifted a lock between two fingers. With a quick snip, the ends fell down on his shoulders.

Neither of them talked while she worked. First, she made some experimental cuts on the front, standing beside him with her knees pressing into his thigh. He fought with his nerves as he reacted to her touch, and breathed a sigh of relief when she finally moved.

Cynthia knew she was getting to Connor. She could see it in the tense set of his shoulders and the alert way he held his head. When he glanced up at her, she saw the flames that burned in his eyes.

Having grown warm, she stripped off his shirt and laid it aside. He was getting to her as well.

She stepped to his right side and layered the hair back from his temple, combing it over his ear until it lay smooth and shining in the overhead light. Aligning his head at a slightly inclined angle, she proceeded around to the back, clipping the dark red curls and letting them fall to the floor.

She liked the shape of his head, the feel of his solidness under her hands. She easily cut off the stray ends along his nape and stepped to his left. After feathering the hair there into place, she circled in front of him again. This time she parted his knees to give her room to stand close as she finished.

Connor thought he was going to explode into pieces. Her light touches were driving him mad. He had never needed a woman so much. Her slightest movement sent floods of desire through his long frame.

His eyes were on a level with the gentle thrust of her breasts. He wanted to rest his forehead between them, to feel her arms around his shoulders as she held him close.

Cynthia forced herself to think only about the job at hand and not of the warmth of his hard thighs so near hers. If she leaned slightly forward, she would be pressed against his hard, male body. She licked her hot, dry lips. She wanted this man as she never had wanted another.

More than mere curiosity drove her; she was a woman answering the call of her nature. She needed him, and he needed the warmth of human contact to remind him that he was a man, a very desirable man.

Finished, she laid the scissors aside. Still standing in the strong semicircle of his thighs, she continued brushing his hair lightly.

"What are you doing to me?" he demanded hoarsely, unable to resist her another moment. He leaned forward, his forehead finding the cushioning embrace of her breasts, and nestled between them, content at last.

His bliss lasted for only a moment, then that wasn't enough—he had to have more of her. He enfolded her slender hips in his arms, drawing her closer until she was pressed against him.

She put the brush on the table, slipped the towel from his shoulders and ran her fingers through his hair, mussing up the freshly styled layers. Neither of them cared. His searching hands roamed her hips and thighs, explored the backs of her knees through the thin material of her slacks.

Weakness overcame her, and she felt as light as a bit of silk caught in the wind. When she trembled, he pulled her down on his lap. He sought her lips, found them and locked them in a kiss that took her breath away.

"I think I'm floating," she whispered when he moved his mouth to kiss her cheek, her chin, her neck.

"Shh—don't talk," he admonished. He stood and carried her into the living room, where the fire still burned merrily. With hands that shook slightly, he laid her on the rug and, kneeling beside her, looked at her for a long time.

"More beautiful than I ever imagined," he said.

He unclipped her hair, pulled the strands loose and spread them on the dark fur until they looked like a pool of honey around her face and shoulders. He moved his hands to her shirt, and she made no protest.

How could she object when she had wanted this from the moment she had watched him chopping wood? She needed him. She needed his gentle touch, needed to find the wealth of tenderness she knew existed in him.

She had no doubts. To make love with him was the only right thing in her life. She lifted her arms, inviting him to come to her.

With a husky murmur, he buried his face in her hair, kissed her a thousand times, basking in her warmth, in the nourishment of her embrace. He needed her more than anything he had ever yearned for.

"Yes," she whispered, encouraging his exploration, letting him touch her as he would, giving everything to him. She was suddenly weightless.

"I've thought of nothing but you for weeks. Your laughter. Your teasing. The way your hair blows in the wind. Your incredible lashes, which guard your eyes—a golden treasure forbidden to ordinary men."

"Not to you," she protested breathlessly as he pushed her unfastened clothing out of the way of his seeking mouth. He caressed her again and again, his hands and lips hot on her skin. She writhed in a kind of tormented ecstasy.

"Cyn," he said, "Cyn," as if her name were a lifeline to a port of safety—only it wasn't.

"You're like a drug," he complained, cupping her breast gently. "I can't get enough."

"Neither can I. I never knew a touch could be so...so compelling." She was filled with the rapture of the moment. "I've dreamed of us like this, in front of the fire while the elements raged outside."

He raised his head, and she felt his fingers tighten slightly on her breast. "Don't confuse this with one of your fantasies," he ordered roughly. "Don't try to read more into it than exists."

"I'm not." She laid her hand over his, caressing the back with the tips of her fingers. But the moment was gone. He pulled away and tucked his shirt into the waistband of his cords.

"There's no use talking to you. Do-gooders hear only what they want to hear."

"And cynics hear only themselves," she responded sadly, sitting up and pulling her shirt closed.

He towered over her. "I hear the truth. Maybe you need to be reminded of it. I was happy here alone—then you invaded my life. If you stay, you'll have to take the consequences. I'm a normal man and, yes, I want to make love to you, but it doesn't mean any more than that. Do you hear me?"

"How can I help but hear? You're shouting."

He swore under his breath. She could confuse the issue faster than anyone he had ever met. "Look, I don't want to hurt you or take advantage of your inexperience. Go save somebody else. I like my life just the way it is."

She couldn't let his incredible misconception go unchallenged. "No, you don't. You wouldn't be fighting so hard if you did. And you wouldn't be warning me if you were as callous as you pretend."

"Don't tell me what I am or am not," he thundered, angry at her insistence in seeing more than existed. He strode out the door into the rain. What did she know about his life? What did she know about him? Only Sister Barnabas had had unquestioning faith in his inner goodness. To everyone else he'd had to prove himself, and even after that, his fiancée, the woman who was supposed to love and trust him, had thought he was capable of crime.

Yet *she*, this woman who had invaded his cabin, insisted she had known all along that he hadn't done it. But she didn't know anything. She was just a trusting do-gooder. What the hell was he going to do with her?

He glared up at the sky; the rain hit him in the face. How long was this storm going to last?

Six

Cynthia looked out the window again. It was dark, and Connor still hadn't returned. She was worried. Perhaps he had gotten hurt, struck by lightning or something. It would serve him right, she decided with perverse humor. Going off and leaving her that way just because he couldn't let himself admit he needed another human being.

She stopped pacing the floor. Maybe that was just as well. Perhaps she wasn't being fair to him. What, after all, did she want from him? An initiation into the rites of lovemaking? Strange, how she had never felt this strongly about another man. While she had complained about men treating her like a kid sister, there had been some who had been interested in her as a woman.

Friends, she decided. She wanted them to be friends. Connor, too, needed someone to talk to, to laugh with, someone who would make no demands on him.

Satisfied with this reasoning, she went into the kitchen to find something to eat. She spied a box of brownie mix on one shelf in a cupboard and powdered eggs on another. She read the instructions on the box. Powdered eggs would work in place of the real thing, she decided.

When the back door opened, she turned toward it with a smile. He was wary as he stepped across the threshold. Did he think she was going to pounce on him? Her smile widened when he looked even more suspicious.

"I've found some brownie mix. Okay if I make a batch?" she ventured.

A short nod was her answer.

Glowering, he strode past her and disappeared into a room off the kitchen. She wondered whether it was his bedroom. Another bedroom opened off the living room, and on the other side of the kitchen were a bathroom and storage closet.

After adding water and powdered eggs to the brownie mix, she beat it with more vigor than called for, poured the batter into a pan and placed it in the oven. Carrying the mixing bowl with her, she went into the living room and sat on the bearskin rug. Using a finger as her utensil, she began to lick the bowl.

"Want some?" she invited when Connor stalked in. He answered her with one cutting glance that said he had no time for tasting brownie batter, no time for her.

She was beginning to find his anger extremely amusing. Fiery bear, she thought as he built up the fire again. He didn't know what to do with her. She threw him for a loop.

He had changed from his wet clothing to fresh jeans and a plaid wool shirt. With the firelight gleaming off his hair and bronzing his face and hands, she realized anew just how good-looking he was. Tough and rugged. Independent. Stubborn. Her smile softened.

She was gripped with a longing to touch him, to run her hands under his shirt and explore the muscular flesh of his back. Staring at him, she ran her finger around the bowl, scooping the chocolate batter into a little ridge that clung to her skin. Just as she was about to taste it, he intercepted her.

Slowly, he lifted her hand to his lips, gazing at her intently. He closed his mouth over her finger and sucked until the sweetness was gone from her skin.

She trembled from the force of her own desire. He moved from her finger to her wrist, running his tongue in lazy circles over the sensitive skin. Her lips parted as she struggled to breathe. She felt as if she were burning up.

"Is this what you want, Cyn?" he asked in deep tones, his eyes never leaving hers. "A physical relationship with no commitment from either of us?"

She touched the damp lock of hair on his forehead, then ran a finger across one brow, down his nose and over his lips. "I don't know," she said quietly.

He sighed and turned away from her, sitting with his legs crossed in front of him. He contemplated the flames leaping over the logs.

She scooped up the last of the brownie mix and licked it off her finger. Setting the bowl aside, she watched him, wondering at his internal battle. "Is it so hard for you to share yourself with another person?" she asked. "Would it be so terrible for us to have this moment with each other?"

He muttered an oath. "How much do you think a man can take? I've wanted you from the moment I looked up and saw you in my yard." He touched her flyaway curls. "With the sunlight in your hair and a smile on your lips, you were a temptation no man could resist."

Cynthia smiled happily. "You're the first man who ever saw me as irresistible. That has to prove something."

"Ha! It proves you've lived your life in a cocoon. Your innocence is enough to turn possible lovers off."

"Does it scare you?" she demanded, not expecting an answer.

Connor's eyes seemed to darken. "Wanting you scares me," he admitted. "There's no place for you in my life. A woman would be a temporary vice to satisfy an appetite."

"I understand." She knew he believed his own reasoning, but she didn't. She had gotten glimpses too many times of the man within to be scared off by his cynicism. "It doesn't matter."

"Of course it matters," he insisted. "You have your life before you. Find yourself a young man, one who's as wet behind the ears as you are. You can grow up together."

"Connor, I'm twenty-five. I've been earning my living for three years now. I haven't slept with a man, but I'm not naive when it comes to men. Why don't you let me decide what I want in my life?"

"Because I see life as it is, not as you'd like it to be."

"Because you're a good man who cares about others," she immediately contradicted him.

He shrugged in exasperation. "You just won't listen, will you? I've tried to warn you, so whatever happens is on your head."

"I'll take responsibility for my actions," she promised solemnly, feeling fiercely tender toward him. The emotion was new and strange . . . and entirely right.

The timer went off on the oven, and she rose to get the brownies. When they cooled enough to cut, she put them on plates and brought them into the living room with glasses of milk. She and Connor ate in front of the fire, sitting on the rug.

"I'm glad you have this bearskin. I've dreamed of making love on it," she said with no thought of hiding her feelings from him or from herself.

He grunted in reply, but she couldn't tell whether or not his response was an agreement. Having gulped down the dessert, she cleaned up the dishes and returned to the hearth, where they leaned against the sofa and gazed into the fire until the night was late. She felt no need for words but let her presence speak to him of a quiet companionship that asked for nothing in return.

Sometime after the rain had slowed to a soft drizzle, she yawned. "I'm going to bed. Where shall I sleep?"

A pained smile curved his attractive mouth. "There" was all he said as he pointed toward the bedroom door.

After washing her face she went to bed, sinking into the feather mattress with a tired sigh. If she was lucky, the storm would last for days.

The rain was coming down in buckets the next morning, she noted with a pleased grin as she dressed and went into the kitchen. Connor was already up, looking extremely handsome. He had apparently decided to adopt a cool, amused attitude toward her.

"Good morning," he said, his glance running over her like an expert judging a good piece of horseflesh. "Sleep well?"

"Yes, I did," she said, flashing him a wide smile. "I smell bacon. Is it ready? I'm starved."

"You must have a hollow leg," he complained, as good-humored as she was determined to be.

"I'll bring you some groceries to replace what I eat," she promised. Glancing around the room, she saw that breakfast was ready. After pouring the coffee for them, she sat down at the scrubbed pine table.

"What was the funniest thing that ever happened to you?" she asked while they ate.

His brows lifted in surprise, but he took her question seriously, thinking for a long time before he came up with an anecdote. "When I was in college, I saved enough money to take this girl out. She was the prettiest one in my English class and came from a wealthy family, so I wanted to take her someplace special. When we got there, I saw the prices were even higher than my wildest imagination. I spoke to the manager. He refused to extend credit, but he said I could help unload a truck and he'd give us our dinner free. So that's what I did." He laughed, and his eyes mellowed as he recalled his youthful triumph. "I finished the job in thirty minutes, twice going back to the table and talking to my date, then excusing myself to make an important phone call. By the time the evening was over, she thought I had business dealings all over the world."

Cynthia laughed even though her heart was hurting for him. "What happened to the romance?"

"We dated a few more times. She didn't like riding rented bikes to the lake for a picnic, and I couldn't afford any more fancy restaurants, so we split."

"I liked picnicking on the pier with you," she said.

"Thanks," he said dryly. "You don't have to feel sorry for me. I'm over the urge to impress females with my man-of-the-world image. They'll have to take me as they find me."

"I will." She gave him an impish grin.

"I wasn't referring to a relationship between you and me."

"Why not? I'm a female; you're a male."

She barely contained her laughter at the chagrin on his face. "You like playing with fire," he warned.

She shook her head. "But I do like touching you." Her gaze went to his hair, which fell neatly into place. "Your hair looks nice. Admit I did a good job," she demanded flirtatiously.

"You did a good job." He finished eating and started cleaning up the kitchen. She helped him, drying while he washed.

"See? Isn't it fun doing things together?" she inquired sweetly when they were done.

His face hardened. "There are other things I'd rather do with you than the dishes," he declared, issuing a challenge that he had no intention of taking on.

"I haven't said no," she said, reminding him that he was the one who had drawn back.

He flicked her backside with the end of the wet dishrag. "Don't tempt me."

Dancing out of his range, she retaliated with the drying towel. "How can I? I'm just a poor innocent who doesn't know a thing about life, remember?"

"Yeah, I remember." He stalked her around the table, his weapon ready. Throwing the towel at him, laughing, she ran for the bathroom, slammed the door and locked it behind her.

Connor picked up the towel and hung it and the dishrag up to dry. He kept hearing the sounds of her laughter as they had chased around the table. He tried to shut out the memory, but it was no use; he knew it would haunt him every day from now on.

It came to him suddenly that he must have played and laughed with Veronica on occasion, but he couldn't remember her laughter. He frowned at an unbidden sense of apprehension and he shook his head. He wasn't going to dwell on it.

He went out on the porch to check the weather. No let-up in the storm, he noted. When he went back inside, he saw a fresh pot of coffee perking on the stove. Cynthia was leafing through a paperback he'd been meaning to read. The scene appeared innocent, domestic and harmless. That was a laugh!

His gaze roamed over her feminine curves. Moodily, he thought that she was a temptation no man could resist, but he wasn't going to get lulled into any intimacy with her. He had learned his lesson well on that score.

Cynthia glanced at Connor, easily detecting hunger for her. "Like what you see?" she teased, preening just a little because he did seem to find her as attractive as she found him. He scowled, and she realized they were somehow back to square one. What had happened to the fun and sharing?

"Did I tell you about the funniest thing that happened to me one time?" she continued when he didn't answer.

"No." He took a step back toward the door. "I need to check on the horses," he stated, and left abruptly.

"Once, Wyatt was determined to kiss me..." she said to the empty room. Her lips trembled, and she stopped.

Connor stayed down at the shed most of the day. Cynthia curled into a corner of the couch and read the adventure novel she'd found. She now wished the storm would let up so she could be on her way. Instead, it seemed to lash the cabin with greater fury.

By the time four o'clock came, she was through with being worried about him, was now angry with him and undyingly resentful. She was calm once more by the time he came in and found her peeling potatoes.

"Hi. I thought I'd mash some potatoes and open a can of green beans to go with a meat loaf I just put in the oven.

Is that okay?'' she asked politely. After all, he was her host.

"Yes, that's fine.'' He hesitated as if about to say more, then walked into the living room. She heard him shoveling the ashes into the scuttle. He emptied the ashes in the backyard and returned in a few minutes, drops of rain clinging to his face and hair.

While she prepared the meal, he built a fire, then went into the bathroom. In a minute, she heard the shower running. When he came out, he wore only his jeans, and she had to look away quickly. He was the most attractive man she had ever seen.

After he went into his room, she forced herself to concentrate on her cooking. She felt the need to show him that she was as competent in the kitchen as he was. He had been making it very clear that he wasn't going to succumb to her charms; she wasn't going to fall at his feet, either.

Firming her lips, she put out the steaming food and set the table. "Dinner,'' she called outside his door.

She took her place and waited until he appeared.

Dressed in khaki slacks and a velour pullover, he looked like a model in a fashion magazine. She glanced down at her outfit in distaste; he had never seen her dressed in anything but pants and shirts. Yet, she mused, he had definitely found her appealing in some ways. He had wanted her—or would any woman do?

She picked up her fork, tasted the meat loaf and immediately looked disgusted. "I forgot the salt,'' she said glumly. So much for impressing him with her culinary talents. She handed him the saltshaker.

"Cynthia,'' he said, haphazardly dashing the salt over his food without tasting it.

She forced herself to meet his eyes. He sounded gravely serious. "Yes?''

"I'm sorry for earlier," he apologized. "I don't want to hurt your feelings, but . . ."

She said nothing as she waited for him to finish his prepared-sounding speech.

"It's been a long time since I've been with a woman, and you . . . well, you're darned attractive." He gave a short laugh. "And I am attracted. But I'm not for you."

She breathed a sigh of relief. So he had been thinking about them. That was good. "Why don't you let me decide that?" she suggested lightly.

"Look," he began again, trying to be reasonable. "You're a sweet person, cute and—"

She threatened him with a fork. "If you call me cute again, I'll fill you full of holes."

She saw that he was taken aback at her fury. A grin tugged at the corners of his mouth as she waved the fork menacingly at his midsection. He hastily leaned back. She continued more softly, "My brother can call me cute, but no one else. Do you understand? I'm not your sister, and I don't intend to act like one. Is that clear?" She rose, flung the fork on the table and stalked off.

He reached out and spun her around before she had gone two feet. "Yeah, perfectly clear," he muttered, lowering his mouth to hers. He kissed her long and hard and convincingly. "Did that seem like a brotherly kiss?" he asked when he stepped back finally, one arrogant brow quirked upward.

She stared at him, dazed. "No," she said, touching her reddened lips. Her smile, brilliant and happy, lit her face.

He realized what he had done. "The rest of what I said still goes. I don't want any entanglements with you or anyone else. Do I make myself clear?" He frowned mightily at her.

She nodded, not at all dismayed by his fierce countenance. "We can still be friends," she told him, guilelessly mocking him.

"Yeah, friends," he said, but he smiled.

Later, they sat in the living room, her on the rug with her back against the sofa, him in the easy chair.

"Would you like to play cards?" she asked.

He shook his head. "I've played enough solitaire during the past year to last me a lifetime," he declared. Then, as if realizing that he didn't want to talk about his life anymore, he shifted uneasily and glanced down at her. "You didn't tell me the funniest thing that ever happened to you," he reminded her.

Cynthia smiled to herself. "Well, Wyatt was chasing me down the street. I had gone to the store for some candy. I can remember to this day I bought redhots, those little heart-shaped candies that are spicy—"

"I know the ones."

"I was on my way back home when he saw me and tried to kiss me again. I got to a fence, and there was a shortcut across the field, but some cows were grazing there. Wyatt was closing fast, and I had to make a decision. I opted for the cows. I was more repulsed by Wyatt's kisses than I was afraid of them."

Connor chuckled, and she paused to smile up at him. "Go on," he said.

"Well, climbing over the gate, I tore my new slacks that Mom had given me for my birthday. They were part of a very expensive matching outfit. Then, about halfway across the field, a bull took offense at my being in his domain. He came over to investigate. It would have been closer for me to go back than to make it to my house, but Wyatt was waiting."

"Definitely a fate to be avoided if possible," he agreed.

She nodded vigorously. "That's what I thought, too. I ran for my backyard, hoping I could make it over the far fence before the bull decided what he was going to do."

"Well?" he demanded when she paused.

She gave him a despairing grin. "You wouldn't believe my luck. I slipped on a slick spot—this was a cow pasture, remember. My new outfit was ruined, simply ruined. At that moment, the bull decided to attack."

"Did he hurt you?" Connor looked worried.

"Wyatt came to my rescue. He yelled and threw rocks, even climbed the gate and came over to help me up after the bull finally ambled off. I was so grateful at not being killed that I threw my arms around him and kissed him, smack on the mouth. Do you know what he did?" she asked indignantly.

"What?"

"He shoved me away, yelled 'Yuk!' and ran off. He never tried to kiss me again. He'd been in love with me for a whole year, but that apparently killed it forever." She clutched her hands to her chest forlornly as she finished her recitation. "And then I had to go home and face my mother. It was her day to have the bridge club."

Connor's mouth twitched, his eyes crinkled at the corners, then his laughter echoed throughout the room. Cynthia grinned up at him. His laughter was the most delightful sound, a full-throated, masculine bellow of amusement.

When he stopped laughing, he got up and knelt on the rug beside her. "It would take more than a fall in a cow pasture to drive me away," he murmured just as his lips touched hers.

Connor exerted iron control and managed to keep the kiss light. Unable to release her, he pulled her onto his lap and held her, rubbing one hand up and down her back. He felt a great, unfathomable tenderness for her. She was still an innocent for all her twenty-five years and mulish streak of independence. He would have to protect her from their desire, and wondered what her family would think of him if they thought he was stripping her of her innocence.

"Did you have a difficult time with your parents when you were growing up? You know, teenage rebellion and all that?" He kept his tone amused.

She answered seriously. "No, actually, I didn't."

"But your brother did?" he asked with quick insight.

She nodded slowly. "My father expected too much from Adam. The only time he paid attention to him was to tell him what he wanted from his son and heir. Naturally, Adam rebelled against everything Dad demanded. When Adam got kicked out of college, Dad sort of wrote him off."

"And your mother?"

"Oh, she was busy with her bridge and social activities. She didn't bother us much. As long as we didn't disgrace her by coming in covered with cow manure." She laughed, her eyes bright with mischief.

Connor laughed, too, but his bent of mind was more serious. There were other ways to abandon children than by leaving them at an orphanage, he thought. The casual neglect of her parents probably caused her to give more to others instead of withdrawing, as he was doing. He wasn't sure who was wise and who was foolish—Cynthia Robards or Connor O'Shaugnessy. But one thing he did know: he liked her, this stubborn young woman with her maddening optimism.

Liking her did not mean he was going to make love to her, though. He had a very strong suspicion she could become a habit that would be hard to break.

She grew heavy in his arms and he saw that she was asleep. Unwilling to let her go, he laid her down on the rug and stretched out beside her, keeping her closer to the fire so she would be warm. After a while, he slept, his body pressed to hers.

Sometime after midnight, he woke. "Cyn, get up. You should be in bed," he whispered, nuzzling his face into her hair.

Her reply was to cuddle up against him with a throaty murmur of contentment. He smiled and gently blew in her ear.

"Don't," she said, her tempting lips pouting. When he moved, she clutched his shirt in a stubborn fist.

"Let me stir the fire," he said, and she relaxed her hold. He got up and added several logs to the fire, then went and took the pillows and quilts off his bed. After making Cynthia and himself comfortable, he lay with her in his arms and watched the flames.

Peace seemed to fill the room, and he realized that he was no longer lonely. A sigh from his bed partner brought his brooding gaze to her face. Kitten face, he thought—the smooth forehead and high cheekbones, the pointy little chin. Mesmerized, he stared at her mouth.

Leaning forward, he kissed her, softly so as not to wake her. She sighed when he lifted his lips from hers.

She made a husky sound, as if demanding more.

He couldn't help himself; her lips were so welcoming. He had to taste them again, had to have that warm honey on his tongue. When her lips parted under his, he sought the inner heat of her, probing her moist sweetness until he was filled with the wonder of her. He had to have more.

He moved his hand to her breasts and explored each until both swelled and hardened. He liked her natural receptiveness to his touch.

Cynthia wakened slowly. Something felt deliciously right, and she was suddenly aware of Connor's lips on hers, his hand on her breast. She pressed closer, wanting that inexplicable something that always eluded her in his arms.

"Mmm," she murmured, encouraging him, wanting him to touch her even more. She pulled his shirt from his pants, then ran her hands over the flesh of his well-muscled back. She felt him shudder slightly.

He made a growling sound deep in his throat as he tore at her shirt. Then he was touching her flesh, searing her with his need.

"I shouldn't do this," he murmured, fighting with his conscience. "I have nothing to give—"

"Yes, you do," she corrected him. "Give me this moment, and I'll be content." Her voice dropped until it was almost inaudible. "I need you."

The last was his undoing. He couldn't resist her. His own needs clamored through his veins, urging him to take what she offered. He lowered his head until their lips met, and then it was too late to think about what was best for her or for him.

His mouth slanted across hers, first one way, then the other, as their lips fused together. His tongue stroked hers, and she responded with a deep kiss that was more than mere flesh against flesh. She thought they shared a meeting of the minds and spirits as well as of their bodies. An unacknowledged but deeply felt understanding united them.

"You're so warm, Cyn," he murmured, kissing along her cheek until he reached her ear. He bit gently on the lobe before moving along the cord of her neck to her throat. "I can't let you go."

"I don't want you to," she assured him, gasping as he took her breast into his mouth, flicking his tongue across her sensitive nipple again and again.

The room had grown warm, and they pushed the covers back. The firelight cast dancing shadows of gold and bronze as they dropped their clothing on the floor. Then there was nothing between them.

Their gazes fondled each other bodily, sweeping in hurried forays over the hard planes and the gentle valleys, trying to take in the totality of each other's bodies, lingering with heated longing on the revealed flesh.

"I've never seen a woman so beautiful," he said in hushed, reverent tones.

She found him equally alluring. With his broad shoulders and narrow hips, his strong flanks and hard-muscled thighs, he was the perfect male. Her gaze skipped from the flaming curls on his head to the wiry hairs on his body. She stared, overwhelmed, at the evidence of his desire for her.

With a sudden chuckle, he held out his arms, and she fell against him.

She didn't know who gasped when they first touched, flesh against flesh. He closed his arms around her, molding her to his hard length as they knelt on the rug.

She raised her arms, wrapped them around his shoulders and clung to him, absorbing his strength, letting him experience her softness, knowing somehow that this was what he needed from her.

He drew back slightly and laid his head on her breasts. For several seconds she and Connor remained still, her hands buried in his hair.

He kissed her again, his lips and hands eager, ravenous in their feasting but never harsh or careless. He searched out her most tender spots and stroked very gently. When his hands meandered over her ribs and glided along her abdomen, she writhed excitedly beneath him.

Her passion drove him to heights he had never reached before. Blood pounded through his ears. Again and again, he warned his clamoring body to be patient. She had to want him as much as he did her.

"Do you like this?" he asked, his mouth near hers while he caressed her hips and thighs before moving to the thatch of dark brown hair at the delta of her slender legs.

"I like everything," she confessed on a breathless whisper. She rubbed her hands seductively over his chest.

He smiled as if he liked her frankness. "You're a natural woman," he complimented her.

She planted a row of kisses over his chest, liking the roughness of his hair on her face. "We all have our pretenses," she told him, feeling wise beyond her years. "I wish we didn't."

She tried to smile at him, but the effort was too great. Her body was aflame with needs that were more demanding than any she had ever known.

"We don't have to pretend about this," he said.

His hands became increasingly intimate until he reached his final goal. She moaned with the pleasure he brought to her and accepted the gift of passion from him. She saw the fires inside her reflected in his eyes and knew he was as excited as she.

"Come to me," she invited him, sure of herself, of them.

"In a minute," he promised. His mouth closed over hers, hot and hungry. He kissed her for several long minutes before he moved.

When he swung easily over her, she opened her legs instinctively and let him nestle within. The tremors of excitement mounted feverishly inside her. He gazed down at her as she dug her nails convulsively into the muscles at his sides. She sensed his struggle. If he left her now, she would never forgive him.

"Do you want me to stop? In another second, there'll be no going back, Cyn," he warned her huskily.

As with the river, there would be no return, she thought. And at the end, would she find her golden dream? Would he? She tightened her arms. "Come to me."

Seven

He began the slow journey that made them one. She had never been so aware of herself or of another person. She exulted in his strength, his control, his gentleness. He was all she had ever imagined a man could be.

"Oh, Connor, it's more wonderful than words can say," she couldn't help telling him.

"You're so easy to make love to. You make a man feel good, as if he were necessary to you."

"You are."

"You feel that way now, but will you tomorrow?" he asked, but didn't wait for an answer. He increased his demands on her, asking for and receiving her willing participation in her seduction. At his slow, gentle thrusts, she responded, instinctively rising to meet his every movement.

The bliss increased to a shining brightness. She was a thread of light, weightless, floating on a dream that was spun out of gossamer strands of delight.

"Yes, oh, yes," she moaned.

He trembled in her arms, and she sensed the onslaught of his uncontrollable passion for her, awed that he could want her like that.

"Cyn, I don't want to hurt you," he whispered raggedly. "But I want you so much."

"It's all right," she soothed, wanting to comfort him. "I want you, too."

The turbulence increased, and she was wafted higher and higher, aware of the smooth flexing of his muscles under her hands, of the blending of their perspiration, of the rising flames in her body as she twisted helplessly beneath him.

She was pulled tighter and tighter until finally the magic thread snapped and she cried out in surprise and tormented ecstasy. Calling his name, she clung to him as she plummeted into a seeming eternity of mindless, star-filled darkness.

With her cry of fulfillment, he thrust deeply into her, and at his release, the final bond was forged between them. Drifting dreamily, she kissed his shoulder and neck while the shudders receded from his body. When he moved beside her, she nestled contentedly against him and listened to the whisper of raindrops against the window. She would always remember this moment, she thought. Always.

A long time later, he spoke. "Was it all you expected?" Tensely, he waited for her answer.

She touched his cheek tenderly. "More."

He let out his breath slowly. "Thank God," he whispered, and closed his eyes as if he was overcome with fatigue.

She smiled. "My fiery bear. My lonesome hermit," she murmured against his chest and drifted into a deep, dreamless sleep.

At dawn, she woke, cold and alone. "Connor?"

"Here," he replied. He brought in an armful of wood, magnificent in his nakedness, and started the fire. He slipped back under the covers, sending shivers through her as he absorbed her warmth. "We'll have to do something to warm you up," he declared, running his hands over her naked flesh.

As he made love to her again, he remembered how he had wanted to hold his hands out to her and warm himself the first time he had met her. Now he knew he had wanted much more; nothing less would have satisfied him.

He filled himself again and again with her, taking her to the brink of ecstasy several times before joining with her as one. It was late in the morning before he remembered to ask her if she had any regrets.

"None," she said.

He stroked her smooth thighs. "You say that now, but wait until the stardust is gone."

"It doesn't have to go, but if it does, I'll live with it."

"You're an idealist." His expression became stern and remote. "You don't know what you're talking about."

"Don't close yourself off from me, not now," she begged softly. "I need you."

He glanced aside, a troubled frown lining his forehead. "That's your biggest mistake—letting yourself believe you need someone else. Take my advice—depend on no one but yourself. Then you won't be hurt."

"The way you were hurt?" she asked. She held on to him when he would have pulled away from her.

"I was a fool. That won't happen again."

"Good. She was the wrong woman for you. You deserve someone stronger." She grinned up at him, her eyes shining.

"Are you that woman?" he challenged.

"I might be," she told him, and grinned impudently.

"You're a temptation I can't resist," he muttered, almost as if he resented that fact.

"Why try?" she asked logically. Running her hands over his shoulders she pressed herself against him, eager for his touch.

"Cyn?" he questioned.

"Yes," she said.

"The horses have to be fed," he told her, leaving their warm nest reluctantly.

"I don't want to move."

"You don't have to. Wait for me here," he invited, his eyes on her slender figure, which was outlined by the covers.

"No, I want to go with you." She pushed the quilts back and stood up, stretching gracefully.

He stole a quick kiss on her upthrust breast. She swatted at him, but he ducked away and pulled on his pants. She dressed quickly in jeans and a shirt, and they went outside to care for the animals.

Ranger snorted and the pack mule grunted in anticipation when Connor entered the shed that he had converted to a stable. Cynthia, following at his heels, noted how clean and neat the place was.

"How can I help?" she asked.

Connor glanced at her. There was a determined gleam in her eye that he was coming to recognize. She'd help whether he wanted her to or not.

"Let's give them some grain. They'll need more energy to help them ward off the cold. Then we'll let them out into the pasture while we clean out the stalls."

"They'll get wet," she pointed out. The rain continued without any signs of a break in the clouds.

He handed her a bucket of horse feed. "They won't mind. Give this to Harry."

"Harry?"

"The mule."

"That's the one I thought you meant." She approached the stall warily. "Will he kick me?"

"Not if you don't get behind him." A grin played at the corners of Connor's mouth as she entered the stall and tried to edge her way past the animal, who already had his head in the manger.

When Harry stamped impatiently, she shrieked and jumped back, slamming the door behind her.

Connor laughed at her, reached over and gave Harry a slap on the backside. The mule reeled around, and glared at them, indignation flashing in his large eyes. "Okay, can see you now. Go on in."

Gathering her courage, she entered the stall, keeping a careful eye on Harry, who kept an eye on the bucket. He stuck his nose in it before she could pour the grain into the bin.

"Smack him," Connor advised.

She gave the animal a tap on the head; he didn't budge. "Harder."

She cast a baleful glance at Connor. "He might take offense."

"You have to show him who's boss." He leaned both arms over the stall and watched, a wide grin on his face.

Taking a breath, she tweaked the mule's ear. With a snort, Harry pulled his head out of the feed bucket, and

Cynthia quickly poured the remainder into the bin and got out of the stall. Resting against the closed door, she sighed loudly in pure relief.

Connor took the bucket from her and refilled it. "Do you want to feed Ranger?"

"Do I have to?" She eyed the eager horse, who was knickering softly, as if urging them to hurry.

"No." Connor lifted her face and studied it. "You're pretty brave...for a girl."

"Give me the bucket." She opened the door, smacked Ranger lightly on the nose, which effectively stopped his foray into the bucket, and dumped the feed into his bin. She returned to Connor's side, handed him the bucket and stalked out of the stable. "I'll see you at the house."

As she crossed the muddy yard to the cabin his laughter trailed after her. She liked the sound of it. Making him laugh was a major accomplishment. Maybe his armor wasn't so thick after all, she mused.

Since the rain soaked her blouse and pants before she got inside, she gave her clothing a quick wash, then she hung them in front of the fire to dry. After a quick shower, she toweled off and went into Connor's bedroom to find something warm to wear in the meantime.

She found his shirt drawer and riffled through it until she found a thick flannel one. As she slid it from the bottom of the stack, she saw a photo underneath. She hesitated, then pulled it out.

The picture was a formal studio print. The kind used for engagement announcements in local papers. He looked handsome in a three-piece suit, and his fiancée was lovely in a silk dress.

She couldn't stop the flash of sympathy that assailed her any more than she could halt the rush of unwarranted jealousy at the sight of them together. For this woman to have had a man like Connor and thrown him away, then to have realized too late what she had lost . . .

"Do you think I should have worn a darker tie?" Connor stood beside her, looking down at the photograph. She hadn't heard him come into the room. "What is this?" he asked when she glanced up at him.

He touched the corner of her eye. She blinked, and a tear slipped onto her lower lashes. He brushed it away.

"Are you crying for me, Cyn?" he asked. His face was unreadable.

She shook her head, giving up the photo when he reached for it. "For her. For what she had and what she lost."

Tearing the picture into halves and then halves again, he swore softly. "Come on."

Pulling on the flannel shirt as she followed him into the living room, she wondered what he was going to do. She stood silently while he threw kindling on the embers in the fireplace and placed the pieces of the ruined photo on top.

"There," he said in satisfaction as the paper curled and disintegrated. "The end of a dream."

"Oh, Connor," she said sadly, compassionately. "It isn't too late. She realized at the end what she had thrown away. She would take you back—"

"She wasn't the dream," he interrupted. "Only the symbol of something that didn't exist in the first place."

"A symbol of what?"

"I don't know," he admitted. His smile was strained. "It doesn't matter. I don't believe in dreams anyway."

Cynthia laid a hand on his arm. "I do. I dreamed of you making love to me on a bearskin rug in front of a fire, and it came true. The reality was even better than the dream."

He swept her up into his arms. "You're a glutton. Did you know that?" He nuzzled her neck until she squealed and tried to struggle free, then he tumbled them both into their bed on the floor. He kissed her until she yielded.

"Take off your clothes," she demanded, unbuttoning his shirt. "You're damp. You need to warm up."

He chuckled as he kissed her throat. "I'm burning up and you know it." His face sobered as he peered down at her. "I want you. Can you take more of this?"

She saw he was seriously concerned about her. She reached for him. "As much as you want to give."

"I might never let you out of this cabin," he warned, teasing again.

"I might never want to leave," she retorted, returning his fervent caresses.

But all good things come to an end, she thought later that day. The last winds of the storm had gone; the thunderheads were dissolving into a light drizzle.

"You asked me earlier if I had any regrets," she murmured, stroking his hair as he lay with his head nestled against her breasts. "There is one. I have to leave. The sky is clearing, and I should be on my way."

"To hell with the mail," he said, tightening his arms around her possessively.

She laughed, delighted with his reluctance to let her go. "I must. You know, the mail must—"

He cut her off with a kiss but finally lifted his head. "It's Saturday. I thought you usually stayed with your brother over the weekend."

"I do."

"Then stay with me," he requested, then moved his lips on her mouth. He kissed her deeply until she had no more thoughts of leaving.

After lunch, as the sun peeked between the clouds he took her outside.

"Where are we going?" she asked. She wore her clean clothes and a wool sweater of his.

"For a ride" was his laconic reply. He walked over to the pasture fence and whistled; both horse and mule came running.

"Have fun," she said, beginning to feel nervous.

"You're coming, too."

"Not me."

"You rode with me to the Gracesons'," he reminded her.

"That was an emergency." She started to back away.

His grin was full of mischief. "Come back here," he said softly.

"Not on your life."

Before she'd gone very far, he hooked an arm around her waist and pulled her back against his body. He nuzzled her neck, tickling her with his stubble until she was helpless with laughter. "Try one lesson. If you don't like it, you can quit." His voice dropped. "Let me give this to you."

She stopped struggling and turned to face him. "All right," she said, suddenly serious.

He saddled Ranger for her and put the packsaddle on the mule for himself. When the animals were ready, he boosted her into the saddle.

"Whoa," she said as Ranger pranced a little.

Connor leaped on Harry. "Settle down," he said sternly to the gelding, who lunged forward, wanting to run.

Leading the way to the meadow, he told Cynthia how to sit, how to hold the reins and how to show the horse who's boss.

"I think he knows he is," she said.

For a long time, they worked in the open field, riding in big circles, then figure eights. After a while, they tried a trot, and then a canter. "That's much better!" she cried.

"If we could just get him from first gear to third without going through second, riding would be easier. Trotting practically knocked my teeth out."

His eyes filled with laughter. "Ready for a ride through the woods?"

She nodded hesitantly, deciding that if Connor thought she could do it, she could. Her "Yes!" was firm.

She and her mount followed Connor and the mule along the path by the creek. The gelding insisted on walking with his nose hanging over Harry's rump, but Harry didn't seem to mind. Little by little, she relaxed and began to enjoy the ride.

The pale sunlight dappled the trail. The creek babbled mysteriously beneath the wind-whipped treetops. Birds rushed about their business before the next storm.

When he thought they had gone far enough, Connor headed back toward the cabin. Throwing his head back, he belted out one song after another in a pleasing baritone all the way home. She joined in. "Down in the valley, the valley so low..."

At the house, he showed her how to unsaddle and care for the animals before they went inside. As they walked across the yard, the clouds were gathering again, blocking out the sun, making the afternoon look like evening.

"This will be a doozy," Connor said, scanning the sky. "Let's put another rope on your plane."

They pulled the aircraft close to the bank and tied it securely, using rubber floats to keep it from banging into the wooden pilings. The storm seemed to have been waiting for them to finish; as soon as they were snug inside, it hit furiously.

"I'm glad you decided to stay," Connor said, holding her in his lap in front of the fire.

"Me, too." There was no place she'd rather be than with him during a storm—or anytime.

"You did well today. I don't think you have to be afraid of horses anymore, do you?" He rubbed her shoulder, causing tremors of desire to run through her.

"Not if I have you along to keep the beast in line," she said. She turned toward him, unable to keep a slight groan from escaping.

"What's that? Sore, are you?" he teased. "We'll have to see if we can't do something about that. Turn over."

He laid her on the sofa and bent over her, massaging her calves and thighs and derriere as he had done before.

"Oh, that feels so good," she said, relaxing completely.

Then, as his hands worked their magic on her, her body became alert as well as supple. Her breath quickened as desire licked along her veins.

"Connor," she whispered seductively.

He bent to her and nibbled on her ear. "Yes, love?" he murmured, amused.

She faced him. "You know what you're doing to me," she accused.

"I hope it's the same thing you're doing to me."

He stretched out alongside her. Through their clothing, she could feel his hard masculinity, and she reached for him passionately.

For a long time, they stayed locked in a deep embrace that excluded the howling of the wind and the pounding of the rain against the windows. Finally, he took her to bed.

"We might as well spend the rest of the afternoon here," he told her as he shed her clothing, item by item, from her slender body. She did the same for him.

Their lovemaking was shared more equally as she gained experience and confidence. He seemed to like whatever she did, whether it was merely looking at his powerful body or running her hands over him or kissing him as he had kissed her.

"Enough," he said hoarsely.

"Not yet. I'm not through," she protested when he pulled her against him and buried his face in the luxury of her wildly tangled hair.

"Rest a minute," he advised. He caressed her breasts in continuous strokes, as if he couldn't bear not to touch her. "You are the most responsive woman. The other men you've known don't know what they've missed."

"I've never wanted anyone but you," she said dreamily. "I wanted to touch you from the moment I saw you. It was the oddest thing—as if it were meant to be."

He stared down at her worriedly. "Don't read more into this than what there is," he warned once more, though not cruelly.

She patted his cheek lightly. "I won't."

His lips came down on hers as if he would obliterate any doubts. She responded to him kiss for kiss until they were gasping for air. With sensuous grace, she moved over him, joining them into one.

She sensed a time in the future when they might not be together, as if her sixth sense anticipated this chapter in her life drawing to a close. It was enough that she had this much for this moment, she thought. For now, this was enough.

Sunday dawned as bleak as the past two days had been. "I'm beginning to wonder if I'll ever get home," she said, surveying the sky from the comfort of his arms as they stood at the window of his bedroom. "Maybe I'll stay forever."

"You'd die of boredom within a month," he predicted.

"Just as you'll turn into an embittered old man." Her smile softened her words.

"Don't you ever give up?"

She laughed out loud. "No." Reaching up, she kissed his scratchy chin. "There's a house-raising in a couple of weeks. Will you go if I stop by for you?"

He scowled. "No."

"Please," she begged mockingly, batting her long lashes at him as an added inducement.

"You're making me repeat myself." He was condescending. "Just leave my life alone. I can get along fine without anyone. You're the one who needs people, not me."

"Everyone needs someone," she said wisely, earning a darker glare from him.

"Not me."

As stubborn as they come, she thought. "I really do have to go as soon as it clears." She sighed softly, regretfully.

By noon, the last of the winds had died away. The massive bank of clouds rolled toward the far horizon, and the sun came out. It was time for her to go.

After insisting that she eat a huge lunch, he helped her check out the plane. It had weathered the storm without mishap. After lifting off, she looked back at him. He was standing on the pier with an arm raised to shield his eyes as he watched her departure. She didn't like leaving him alone.

Their time together had been special. The magic had been there for her, and she was sure it had been for him, too, if he would only admit it. He had let her come close for those few hours, and he hadn't gotten angry at her for opening his dresser drawers to find a shirt, nor had he seemed upset at her looking at the photograph.

The other woman, she mused. Did she see his former fiancée as a threat to any lasting relationship between them? She hadn't been able to decipher his reactions when he burned the photo, but she thought it indicated he was putting the past behind him for good. If so, that was a step in the right direction.

"I'll turn you into a teddy bear yet," she promised as she lifted above the thick trees and met the full brightness of the afternoon sun. She was humming happily when it was time for her to identify herself and ask for landing instructions back at her home base.

Eight

Someday I'll fly you through Hell's Canyon," Cynthia promised. "It's impressive."

"I'll bet," Connor said, still looking at the panoramic view below the plane.

She glanced over at him. He was wearing jeans and a cotton shirt, appropriate attire for the house-raising. His toolbox was stored in the cargo space behind them. Pride and a desire to show him off swelled her heart. It had taken her a long time to talk him into comimg, but she had been very persuasive last night.

"What does that satisfied grin imply?" he asked, playfully pulling her flyaway hair.

"That I enjoyed convincing you to attend the party," she informed him.

His smile faded as he recalled the previous evening. "I thought you spent Friday nights with your brother," he had said when she arrived, a bag of groceries in hand.

"I've been over to his place and left him a note," she had explained. "Shall I go back?" There was a challenge in the tilt of her chin.

"And if I said yes?"

She had considered. "I'd probably stay anyway."

He had been unable to resist taking her into his arms. "Then there's no use in my saying it, is there?" They had spent the night in his bed.

He drew a deep breath and let it out slowly. The past two weeks had been the longest of his life. He had found himself watching for her every day, even when she wasn't expected. Yesterday, he had given in and tied a red neckerchief to the mailbox and put a note inside inviting her to lunch. She had landed exactly at twelve, then had come back at five, when she'd finished her route. When he had demanded to know why she hadn't been back before then, she had told him she had received no invitation. Stubborn...

"Why the heavy sigh?" she asked.

He smiled. "I was thinking about last night and wondering how I let myself be talked into doing a hard day's work."

"This is a party. It's going to be fun. You'll see," she promised.

"It was fun having you to myself," he complained soulfully.

She liked their joking, and basked in their happiness. She didn't let herself think ahead to a time when he would be gone.

"Here we are. Hold on—this is a difficult turn."

She expertly banked and brought the plane in for a landing on a bumpy meadow. Several people waved to them from the shade of the trees as they coasted to a stop and hopped out. She pulled Connor along by the hand to meet them.

"This is Connor O'Shaugnessy. He bought the old Taylor place," Cynthia told them all.

Ralph and Trudy Jones welcomed him and thanked him for coming to help out. Peter and Ann Graceson were there; they shook hands and told of the rescue of their nephew. There were three other families, two with young children, the other with teenagers, who crowded around to meet the newcomer.

"Here's my brother," Cynthia exclaimed when Adam pulled in to the clearing in a four-wheel-drive vehicle. She quelled her apprehension as he came over to them. "This is Adam," she said. "Adam, this is Connor."

It didn't take a lot of intuition for her to know that Adam was angry. She guessed the cause; he knew where she had stayed last night. But she had never cautioned him about his choice of dates, and he would have to allow her the same discretion.

Connor perused the group. "I didn't realize so many people lived in the mountains," he said to Adam and the Gracesons, who had claimed him as a special friend.

"Most people are summer residents," Peter explained. "You and Adam are the only ones here who plan to stay the year. There are a couple of newlyweds over the next hill who are trying to farm and run a few head of cattle. I don't expect them to last past Christmas."

"Don't be such a pessimist," Ann chided him.

"All right. I'll give them until spring," he conceded, chuckling as his wife made a face.

Cynthia thought of spending the winter in the cabin with Connor. She knew she couldn't, but it was an exciting idea. To go tramping through the woods with him, to lie on the rug and be enveloped in the silence of a snowfall . . .

She realized the others were looking at her. "I'm sorry. I was lost in a daydream. What did you say?"

"Ralph says it's time to start," Adam told her, his eyes narrowed on her and Connor.

The site had been blocked out and the foundation laid for the cabin, which would consist of a large room and a small one. The fireplace was already built—the chimney looked funny standing by itself—and would occupy one end of the large all-purpose room. The smaller room was the bedroom with a tiny bathroom.

Everyone worked, following the printed instructions that had come with the kit. When Connor explained what some of the directions meant, he was elected the foreman of the project. From there the work proceeded smoothly.

The group completed each of the four walls and laid them on the ground next to their final position. With a hoist and pulley and several pairs of willing hands, they raised each one into position and bolted it into place.

For Cynthia, there was something basically satisfying in raising a house. It symbolized the putting down of roots. Her gaze went to Connor, who was looking over the next set of instructions.

He glanced toward the house, looking briefly at her. She felt herself going warm inside as she recalled their shared intimacy. Her face was glowing as she met the penetrating glance of her brother.

"Time to eat," Trudy Jones called out. She gave the teenagers directions on how to make a table with boards and two sawhorses. Four men were dispatched to bring up the beer and soft drinks that had been cooling in the creek while everyone else, down to the three-year-old, was given various tasks.

Peter manned the grill, and soon they were eating barbecued chicken and hamburgers along with potato chips, beans and pickles. Connor settled next to Cynthia with a heaping plate.

"Good grief, did you leave anything?" she asked.

"There's enough for seconds," he assured her, eyeing her plate, which was also stacked pretty high. "You won't starve," he remarked wryly.

She grinned and leaned back on a tree trunk. Around them in a loose circle, the others sat in lawn chairs, on the grass or perched on a fallen tree. Adam had a teenager on one side and a ten-year-old on the other, both female. He was entertaining them, and obviously had them charmed.

"Adam is okay now," Cynthia murmured to Connor. "Doesn't he look happy?"

Connor studied the small group. "Most men are happy with adoring females at their feet."

"Don't go cynical on me," she admonished him abruptly. It was too perfect a day for him to annoy her with his cool observations.

"This isn't real, Cyn." He was suddenly harsh, as if it were important to him that she see life clearly.

"What isn't?" she asked quietly.

He waved a hand around the pleasant scene, taking in the couples and families, one mother rocking a three-year-old in her arms as he drowsily fought off an afternoon nap.

"These aren't pioneer times. Building a cabin in the woods is just a romantic notion now, not a necessity."

"That's true. What's wrong with romantic notions?" Her eyes softened. "I thought you were pretty romantic last night."

His hungry perusal promised more of the same. "Maybe it's just that I'm willing to give you what you want in order to get what I want," he said cryptically.

She laughed and shook her head. "You're a wonderful lover, Connor, considerate . . . wildly exciting. But you're more than that. You're a person of character and strength."

He sighed as if he were giving up on convincing her of reality. "My ego is growing by leaps and bounds," he warned her, a sparkle igniting in the jade depths of his eyes. He touched her cheek before picking up a piece of fried chicken. Across the small clearing, his gaze met her brother's.

"I missed you last night," Adam said to Cynthia when he got a moment alone with her that afternoon. They had volunteered to go to the creek for more cool drinks.

"I left you a note. Didn't you see it?"

"Yeah. Where did you stay?"

She hesitated a second. Better to get the truth out in the open than to skirt around it, she decided. Adam knew it anyway; he just wanted confirmation. "With Connor."

"That's what I figured. So now that you're involved with him, what's next?"

She loaded a basket with several cans of beer and cola. "I don't know," she answered thoughtfully. "I'll just have to take each day as it comes. I hope he goes back to work soon. This long absence can't be good for him."

Adam snorted. "I don't give a damn about what's good for him. What about you? What will you do when he leaves?"

She leaned her head on his shoulder. "Cry," she suggested with a trace of rueful amusement. She looked up at him. "I'm a big girl. I'll have to take my chances."

He ruffled the curls that had fallen over her forehead. "He's not good enough for you."

"He's what I want," she swore fiercely. The full implication of her words hit her.

Adam picked up a twig, broke it into bits and dropped the pieces into the running water. "You're in love with him."

When she didn't say anything, Adam picked up the basket, and they rejoined the others.

At six, the group had finished for the day. The floor was in, the walls were up and the roof was on. The family could finish the rest of the work at their leisure.

"A nice summer project for them," Cynthia observed to Adam as they neatly stacked odds and ends next to the cabin.

"Don't rush off," Trudy yelled to her guests. "There's supper and dancing."

The festivities started as Peter grilled the steaks that Cynthia had flown in the day before. Wine was uncorked and poured freely. After dinner, Peter brought out his guitar and played old, familiar cowboy songs. Later there was dancing.

Cynthia turned expectantly to Connor. He was looking at her, his eyes warm with emotions she couldn't quite read. He took her lightly into his arms.

"This has been a nice day, hasn't it?" she said happily. Adam and Connor had gotten along well after they'd sized each other up. Watching them consult each other as they worked, she had known that Adam had read her right; she was in love, she knew now.

"Yes."

"Are you ready to leave? We probably should be getting along. I won't be able to land after it gets dark." She grinned up at him. "I'd have to kidnap you and take you home with me."

"Let me dance with my hostess first," he requested.

They stayed another fifteen minutes, during which time Connor danced not only with Trudy but with the teenager who had sat next to Adam during lunch. She seemed to have switched her interests to Connor. Cynthia battled with her jealousy and lost. She hated anyone else in his arms—and the girl was practically glued to him.

"It's time to go," she said to Adam when he sauntered over to her and dropped an arm over her shoulders.

"Yes. I'm going to hit the trail, too. I want to get an early start in the morning." His voice dropped to a whisper. "Your lame duck is all right."

Her face lit up at his approval. "Thanks. How's the mine coming?" She realized she hadn't been down in it in days. "Where are you digging now?"

"I've broken through into the old shaft, but I haven't found the original opening. Right now I'm shoring up the old timbers—some of them are pretty rotten. There's been heavy water penetration on that side."

A worried frown creased her forehead. "Be careful."

He gave her a squeeze. "Don't worry. I'm always careful."

"Ha!"

He pulled her hair, and she poked him in the ribs, laughing brightly, her serious mood broken. Adam walked her to the plane, giving her a list of supplies to bring on her next trip.

Connor followed a few steps behind the brother and sister, suddenly feeling left out. They had shared a lifetime with each other; naturally they were close. Whatever troubles they had, they confided them to each other and faced them together.

Frustration washed over him, leaving him confused. Only a few short weeks before he had been at peace, and now he'd been thrown off balance, threatened by emotions he didn't want to feel.

This house-raising, pioneering stuff was getting to him. Construction had been his career. He missed working with tools and materials, missed the contact with friends as they built something together they knew would last longer than they would.

In his imagination, he kept seeing scenes from a fantasy—him and Cyn, carving out a place in the wilderness...

Her voice interrupted his dream. "Coming?"

She turned to him and held out her arm. He took the few steps that would put him in her embrace. An arm around each of the two men, she walked briskly toward the plane. In a few minutes, she and Connor were taking off into the evening sky.

"Can you see well enough to land?" he inquired.

"I'd better be able to—else we're in trouble." She laughed when he cast her a chastising look. "I think I could fly these hills blindfolded."

"Not with me in the plane."

"Coward."

"Coward?" He lifted one sardonic brow.

"Well, if the shoe fits..." She gave him a challenging glance, then turned her attention to the tricky landing on the dark surface of the lagoon. She brought them up to the pier without so much as a jolt.

After they secured the plane, Cynthia hummed as they walked up the path. She slipped her arm around Connor and laid her head against him. "Did you enjoy your last dance with that teenage Lolita?" she asked, trying her best to sound nonchalant.

"She was cute" was all he said. He stopped and faced her, his hands on her shoulders as he held her still and studied her face in the faint light. "You're beautiful."

He lifted her into his arms and carried her inside. He moved his hand on her body urgently as he removed her clothing. He kissed her lips, then her breasts, as if he couldn't get enough.

"Help me take your clothes off," she whispered, shaken by the intensity of his desire.

He released her just long enough to get undressed with her aid. Then he took her to bed.

He lay beside her and stared down at her for a long time, his large hand running from her neck to her thighs, over and over, until she made a little sound of protest.

"Do you want more than this?" he asked, his voice strained and husky.

"Yes. I want you," she breathed, her heartbeat increasing with each caress.

"Why, Cyn?" he asked, but he didn't let her answer. He covered her mouth in a passionate kiss that totally disrupted her ability to think.

He encircled her with his arms, holding her so close that she could feel the rapid beat of his heart against her breasts. He moved his body over her, crushing her, pressing his hips against her again and again, reminding her of his intense male desire until she was on fire for him.

But he wouldn't take her. Instead, he explored her slender loveliness as if discovering it for the first time, as if her very form were a strange and new delight that filled him with wonder.

"You are the most exquisite woman," he whispered.

She savored his compliments, storing each one in her heart. His lips roamed her face and neck, down the center of her chest. He caressed each breast until she demanded his lips on hers.

He moved his mouth over her body, exploring the outline of her rib cage beneath her satiny skin. When he reached her navel, he delved into it until she rolled away from him laughing. He caught her, pulled her back and started over, from her lips to her neck, to her throat, her breasts, the taut flesh of her abdomen, her thighs.

With his lips he found each pulse point of sensitivity until he discovered the most sensitive one of all. With gentle hands, he held her captive to the most intense desire she had yet known, then stroked her legs, hips, and her breasts.

She felt the world spinning out of control as he brought her to increasing heights of ecstasy. She murmured his name, first in a whisper, then in a cry as the golden thread snapped and the world disappeared in a shattering rainbow.

"Connor!" she cried, collapsing into stillness.

He gathered her into his arms and held her for an eternity. Then he began again. The passion rose more swiftly this time, and she was aware of his desire rising with hers. He entered her, moving with her movements, meeting her needs and adding his own until the wildness was more than either of them could stand. They rode the wild rapids of the enchanted river and finally came to the peaceful bay of contentment.

Cynthia encircled his neck and pulled him to her for one last kiss before he left her. She was filled with the rapture of their lovemaking. "I love you," she vowed. "I love you."

Even before he stiffened in her arms, she knew she had said the wrong thing, but there was no taking back the words.

He raised his head.

She met his look with defiance in her gaze. "I do," she said before he could reply.

He got up, found his jeans and pulled them on. She watched him with a sinking heart.

"You don't know what you're saying. You're confusing illusion with reality," he advised, his voice carefully low and even. "That make-believe nonsense today was powerful, I'll admit. I even felt a sentimental twinge or two. But it was a lie."

"Love—"

"—is a myth," he finished for her. "You'd get over it quick enough as soon as life didn't go smoothly."

She shook her head. "Not me. I love forever, through thick and thin, rain, snow, sleet and all that stuff." She smiled up at him bravely as he started for the door.

"There's no use talking to you. You have the answer to everything." With that, he walked out.

"No, I don't," she called to his retreating back. "I don't have a clue to you."

Lying alone in the bed, she wondered if she had totally destroyed her chances with him. Well, it couldn't be helped.

She heard him outside. Where was he going? It was dark, and getting cold. She waited, her nerves stretched thin. Finally he returned, went into the other bedroom and closed the door.

Furious and frustrated, she settled back against the pillows. Maybe that was just as well. Now that he knew how she felt, he was going to have to deal with that fact. Her love, whether he wanted it or not, was proof that she wanted more from him than exciting nights.

But she would accept his lovemaking for now. It was a beginning.

At dawn, she dressed to leave and went into the kitchen. He was at the table, a cup of coffee in front of him. He looked as if he hadn't slept at all. Surprisingly, she had slept very well.

"Good morning," she said cheerfully. Mornings always filled her with hope—a new day, a new start.

He looked at her, his expression as detached as it had been the first time she had seen him. Well, she had gotten beyond his defenses before, she reminded herself.

"Good morning," he said warily.

"Would you like some bacon and eggs? I think I'll have some." When he refused her offer, she prepared enough for herself. Taking her usual place at the table, she ate calmly, cleaned up her dishes and gathered her belongings. "I've got to go," she announced.

"All right." He stood and walked with her out to the plane.

She began to get nervous; his silence was deafening. "I'll see you Tuesday."

He shook his head. "I think it would be better if you didn't." He gazed into the distance, his face seemingly etched in granite.

"Why?" She refused to be daunted. She had expected something like this.

"Because."

"Why are you retreating from me again?" she asked quietly.

He made an angry gesture, as if he was about to forcibly send her away. "Dammit, quit prying. You're not my therapist. I told you I didn't want an involvement. I wanted to be alone, to rethink my life and figure out where I'm going. I don't need any extra complications."

"My love doesn't change anything between us. It doesn't complicate anything."

"Doesn't it?" He gave a mocking laugh. "Don't you think I have any conscience at all? I have nothing to give you."

"Except yourself," she said.

She saw him swallow with difficulty before he spoke. "Find yourself a man who will appreciate your virtues. You're a beautiful woman. It shouldn't be hard. You deserve that much."

Cynthia climbed into the plane without further argument. She thought of her fellow worker who had been a thief. She had been wrong about him. She had felt sorry for Mr. Taylor when his family had moved him against his wishes to the retirement home. She had been wrong about him; he was much happier where he was.

Perhaps she was wrong about Connor, too. Perhaps he didn't need her interference in his life. He was a man. He could make his own decisions without her help.

She pushed back the curls that blew across her temples and felt infinitely weary. "Thanks." She managed a teasing smile. "I won't bother you anymore. I promise."

He caught her hand before she closed the door. "Do you hate me?" he demanded.

"No, of course not."

He nodded and stepped back, untying the painter for her.

She started the engine. As she lifted into the air a few seconds later, she saw him walking toward his cabin, his stride angry, as if he would have liked to strike someone. She quelled her concern for him. If he was alone and angry, that was his choice. She felt angry herself.

Love was not a miracle cure. Neither was it a myth. She hoped Connor would discover that again someday. She hoped that someday she would, too.

Nine

It was almost two o'clock on Tuesday before she landed in the meadow near Adam's cabin. Her day had been busy—everyone on the route had had a letter, including Connor. She had put his correspondence—a letter from his attorney, according to the return address—in the box without seeing any sign of him. In fact, she hadn't seen him in almost three weeks.

That was just as well, she thought as she walked across the springy grass toward the mine. She wasn't going to worry about him. He had been right; she was a busybody. She had talked to Mr. Taylor, and his gentle chiding had made her see that she involved herself in other people's business entirely too much. But no more, she promised herself. From now on she would do her job and not intrude on anyone's life.

"Adam?" she called, switching on the flashlight she always carried. She ventured into the mine and began to follow the trail of arrows into the narrow opening.

There was no answer, but then, she hadn't really expected him to be working this close to the surface. She walked on, noting the work he had done on the interior since the last time she had been down into the shaft. New timbers shored up crumbling granite columns, and she marveled at the tremendous amount of effort it must have taken for one man to have done the work by himself. If only she could find something for him that he liked as well as mining...

"No," she said aloud, reminding herself of her vow not to interfere.

It wasn't until she had gone all the way to the opening into the original mine that she started to feel apprehensive. She should have heard or seen some signs of him by now. "Adam," she called. *Adam!*

Only the echo of her voice greeted her. The hair stood up on the back of her neck. Her heartbeat was loud in her ears; the silence was unnerving.

Plastic arrows in Day-Glo orange marked her brother's course into the old shaft, with its rotten timbers and signs of cave-ins. She bent to step through the low opening, swinging her flashlight from side to side.

She walked along the debris-strewn trail deep into the mountain. The air was musty and a dry dust covered everything, turning her shoes a ghostly white. Occasionally, she spotted a glistening surface where water had seeped into the chamber, the evidence of nature's relentless work.

She crossed two passages, following the arrows that clearly marked the way. Hesitantly, she continued, drawn deeper and deeper into the mountain by a growing anxiety that all was not well. When she came to an arrow, her relief was so great that she had to pause to let her pulse slow down before proceeding. Her serenity was short-lived, however. A few yards along the way, she found what she had been dreading—a cave-in, recent and serious.

"Adam?" she called.

She put her ear against the wall next to the rocky talus. Nothing. Only the steady drip of water farther along the tunnel. A shiver raked along her spine.

"Adam," she yelled.

"Adam . . . Adam . . . Adam," the echo repeated endlessly.

She began to pray, knowing her worst fears were realized. He was trapped inside the cavern, possibly hurt. He had to be hurt, or else he would have answered.

Her thoughts were disjointed, chaotic. Taking a tight grip on her emotions, she decided to investigate the cabin and grounds before sounding the alarm. Maybe he had forgotten to pick up the arrows when he'd left. Maybe he had gone hunting that morning, instead of going into the mines.

"And maybe pigs fly," she muttered as she hurried to the cabin.

It was empty. His gun was hanging over the door. The mining tools that he usually stashed in the corner were missing. There was no denying the fact that he was in the mine. She had to get help.

"Connor," she whispered, looking toward his cabin. She ran to the plane and took off. Once she was in the air, she put out a call for help and reached the owner of the grocery store and fish camp near the Graceson place. He assured her he would telephone for help immediately. She gave directions and signed off.

Five minutes later, she landed and tied up at Connor's pier. Please let him be here, she prayed as she ran up the path. "Connor," she called, opening the door and rushing into the cabin. He wasn't there.

She went out back. He was down by the shed, chopping firewood. He would have enough to last through two seasons of blizzards, she thought inanely as she ran to him.

He saw her from the corner of his eye and twisted around to face her, his stance wary, his face unwelcoming. She stopped a few feet away.

"Adam's in trouble," she said. "I think...I'm sure he's trapped in the mine. There's a cave-in where he's been exploring."

"Have you called for help?" he asked.

She nodded. "Yes, I got hold of John Waterson at the general store. He'll phone the forestry service. They'll send help." She was breathless by the time she finished. Her hand went to her pounding breast, as if it could still the tremor inside her. "Come," she said. "You must come."

"I'm not a mining engineer, Cyn," he said, choosing his words with care.

She brushed his warning aside. "I'm not asking you as an engineer. I'm asking for your help as one human being to another. My brother is in trouble. I need your strength to help me dig him out. We might be able to break through, to provide him with fresh air before help arrives. Before it's too late."

Connor saw he had no choice. If the mine collapsed due to some mistake on his part, she would hate him, but there was no way he could refuse and betray the trust in her eyes.

"Fly back to the mine and wait for me. I'll get some gear together and ride over. We might need the horses to help us shore up some timbers."

"Good idea." She hugged him and rushed off.

He went to the tack room and removed Ranger's saddle from the hook. What would he need? A pick, the ax, his tools . . . rope. Food? He'd throw some in, he decided.

In fifteen minutes, he was on the trail leading around the alcove. The path wound across the shallow ravine and up toward higher peaks. It was going to be a long ride. He urged Ranger into as fast a pace as he dared. The mule followed complacently.

Cynthia hopped out of the plane before the engine stopped turning over. She had talked to Mr. Waterson and found out the rescue operation was under way. A mining expert would be flown up from a road-tunneling project he was working on.

"He's one of the best in the country," Mr. Waterson had assured her. "The ranger said he went to that college over in Montana for mining engineers."

"Good. I'm going to start removing some of the debris."

"You ought to wait for the expert," he had cautioned.

"No, I'm going ahead," she had insisted.

A few minutes could make a difference between life and death, she reasoned now as she looked around the cabin for some tools. She found a broken spade and a wheelbarrow and headed for the mine.

She soon discovered that the spade was worthless. It was faster to use her hands to load the rocks into the wheelbarrow and take them to the surface. The work was incredibly difficult. She was exhausted after one trip and had to decrease the load in order to get the next one up the inclined tunnel. Periodically she called Adam's name but got no reply.

An hour later, she staggered to the top, emptied the wheelbarrow and flopped down on the grass. She couldn't lift another rock. Her muscles burned with fatigue, and her arms and legs were shaking so badly, the wheelbarrow had nearly rolled back on her as she had struggled to the entrance.

Through the hard ground next to her ear, she heard the staccato sound of hoofbeats. She sat up just as Connor rode into sight across the meadow.

He leaped from Ranger's back and strode toward her. "Any news?" he asked in his deep baritone.

She shook her head and nearly fell into his arms.

He held her against him, worried by her appearance. He could feel her trembling. "You need to rest," he began.

"No, I couldn't," she protested, her words muffled against his chest. "We have to hurry."

"Show me where you think he is. Leave that," he said when she went to the wheelbarrow.

"We'll need it." She stubbornly gripped the handles and started down the shaft.

"Let me get my things," Connor requested, then removed the items he had brought and tied the two mounts to a low tree. He deposited the tools in the wheelbarrow and took the handles. "Lead the way," he ordered, but his tone was gentle.

They walked in silence to the place where she had been digging. Her efforts were pitiful when compared with the pile of fallen dirt and rocks, and he had to swallow hard against the sudden obstruction in his throat.

"Here it is." She pointed.

"Have you tried calling to him?"

"Of course."

"Let's see if we can rouse him." He selected his hammer from the toolbox and knocked on the wall twice. They waited but received no response. Working systematically, he made his way along the cavern, tapping on the wall.

Cynthia walked along beside him, or behind him if the opening wasn't wide enough. "He wasn't up this way, according to the direction of the arrows," she told him as he searched along a different branch of the mine.

"We don't know how the old mine runs. It may have a side tunnel near this one like the shaft where he broke through."

Connor continued walking and tapping and listening. As they neared a dead end, he stopped and tapped again, the metallic *clink* of the hammer against stone setting her nerves on edge. She was impatient to get on with the digging.

"Let's go back—"

"Shhh," he said, holding up a hand to her. He tapped again and listened.

She didn't hear anything. Her amber eyes gleamed with impatience. "Connor—"

Just then, into the harsh silence of the cavern came an unmistakable *thunk-thunk* in reply. Cynthia froze, not even daring to breathe. Connor tapped twice. The answer immediately sounded through the stone.

"He's up this way," Connor said. "Is there another entrance to the mines?"

"No . . . yes! There might be. I mean, there must have been at one time, but Adam said he hadn't been able to find it. Do you think he could be close to it?"

Connor shrugged. His frown dampened her sudden enthusiasm. "I don't know, but if we could find the other entrance, we might be able to clear it and guide him to it."

"Yes, let's do that. Oh, hurry, please hurry." She turned and led the way at a near run to the surface. A helicopter was circling overhead. She waved the flashlight at it. In a moment it had set down, and passengers climbed out. "Thank God. Help has arrived," she quavered.

"Yes," Connor said, standing beside her. "Thank God."

Hearing the relief in his voice, she looked up and laid a hand on his arm. "I'll never forget that you were here first," she said softly.

He shook her hand off. "It was the only thing to do," he said almost curtly, and walked over to help unload the chopper.

In the ensuing confusion, Cynthia forgot about his brusqueness. She recognized Ted MacCormick, the head of the ranger service in the area, and went over to where he and Connor were discussing the rescue.

"Cynthia, we're in luck," the ranger said, squeezing her hand comfortingly between both of his. "The best mining expert in the States was down at the Big Creek project, giving us some advice. I brought him along. Here he is."

Cynthia smiled as a young man came over to them. He was blond and extremely good-looking. His pleasant but serious countenance exuded an air of confidence that she instinctively trusted.

"Cynthia," the ranger said, "this is Wyatt Carter."

Her eyes widened in surprise. For a suspended moment, she could only stare at the man, then she laughed and threw her arms around him. "Wyatt!" she cried. She felt a little hysterical with happiness. Wyatt had saved her from the bull; he would save Adam from the mine.

"Do I know you?" Wyatt asked good-naturedly, but perplexed.

"I'm Cynthia. Cynthia Robards. You rescued me from the bull when I was nine years old."

His eyes widened in amazement. "Cynthia!" He held her away from him and looked her over. "All grown-up," he said, approving of what he saw. "What are you doing here?"

She recovered her poise. "Adam is my brother. He's the one trapped in the old mine shaft. Connor—" she held out a hand to him, pulling him forward "—got a response from Adam just a few minutes ago, so we know he's alive. We don't know if he's hurt, though." She gazed at Wyatt as if he were a miracle worker.

He patted her on the shoulder. "We'll get him out," he promised in a deep, quiet voice.

Connor was startled at his anger as he watched Cynthia respond to Wyatt's reassuring presence. The man exuded confidence. He was certainly no down-and-outer who appealed to her tender heart. He was more dangerous than that.

Wyatt Carter had been in love with Cynthia when he was ten years old; at twenty-six, he seemed to be smitten all over again. And he was the hero sent in to rescue her beloved brother. That was surely a combination no woman could resist, and the way she was staring at him with her amber eyes shining indicated that she had no intention of resisting. Connor suppressed his ridiculous hostile emotions and listened to the conversation.

"We'll use the sonar to determine where the connecting wall is thinnest," Wyatt said. "We'll cut through at that point."

"If we could find the old entrance," Connor put in, "that might be faster."

Wyatt looked at him. "There's another entrance?"

Connor nodded. "Probably. Adam broke through into an old mine that apparently wasn't part of the one he was working in, which was newer." He looked at Cynthia, who confirmed his conclusions. "I'm not sure about cutting through. His position sounded a good distance from the breakthrough."

"Let's go down there and check it out," Wyatt said, claiming Connor as an ally. The two men hurried off.

"I'll come, too," Cynthia said, following.

Wyatt faced her. "I think it would be better if you stayed up here, out of the way."

"I know those mines as well as Adam," she protested.

"Wyatt's right." Connor hooked a hand around her neck and massaged the tight muscles there. He was gripped by a need to assert his right to touch her in front of the childhood friend. "You don't know anything about the section Adam is in. Let the expert do his job." He nodded in Wyatt's direction, giving the man his due.

She was comforted by the look of understanding in his eyes. He knew she wanted to be in the thick of things. Resigning herself to patience, she agreed with a slight nod.

"Start some soup if you have the ingredients," he advised. "Adam will need something warm and nourishing when he comes out." He made her feel better with his air of confidence in the rescue team.

"Yes, I will." She watched as Wyatt called to two other men and the four of them started down into the dark mine wearing miner's hats with lanterns attached.

"I'd better see about setting up a kitchen," Ted mentioned. "These men will need food."

Cynthia helped after a large tent was pitched next to the cabin. She set out a variety of sandwiches, fruit and snacks. Cots were placed in one end of the tent so the men could rest.

"You seem to think you'll be here awhile," she said to Ted as she distributed blankets. Her voice broke slightly.

His gaze was sympathetic. "These mine rescues can take a few days."

"I see." Worry gnawed at her insides. She was tired, but her body was tense and restless, making it impossible for her to sit down.

"But with the power equipment we have nowadays, it usually goes a lot faster," he added hastily, bringing a faint smile to her pale face.

She went into Adam's cabin and gathered the ingredients for a large pot of vegetable soup. When it was simmering, she drifted outside to watch.

Trudy and Ralph Jones drove into the clearing. "We heard your call on the radio. We've come to help," Trudy called as they stopped.

She and her husband unloaded from their Jeep a case of soft drinks, several packages of chips and a huge cake.

"We were going to ask you to pass the word and invite everyone to a party at the end of the month to see our house. It's almost finished. I decided to bake the cake and bring it and the other stuff over here in case this takes a while." She squeezed Cynthia's hand. "But I'm sure they'll have him out in no time."

Cynthia managed to smile and thank them for coming. What she had thought would take hours, everyone else seemed to think might take days. Her spirits dropped to their lowest level.

"Have you heard anything?" Ralph asked.

Cynthia brightened. "Yes, Connor got an answer when he tapped on one of the walls."

"That's good news." Both husband and wife looked relieved.

As the afternoon wore on, more people arrived, bringing food and any tools they thought might be useful. Soon most of the population of the area, including the two newlyweds, were present and demanding to be allowed to help.

Ted MacCormick, the official head of the rescue, consulted with Wyatt and Connor and set up a sweep operation to search the entire area for the old mine shaft. Everyone was assigned a section and sternly told to maintain sight with the next person down the line. Cynthia, Trudy, Ann Graceson and the bride, Susan, were asked to stay at the main tent and coordinate the efforts of the individual teams. They pored over maps and marked out the sections as each was explored.

As the light faded, the four women made sure everyone was called in and accounted for. They served the troops hot soup and sandwiches for supper.

Wyatt had decided to open up a section of tunnel at a point between the two mines that seemed less rocky than the rest. He didn't think the rescuers could take a chance on blasting their way through, since they didn't know the condition on the other side.

"Why can't you clear out the fallen rock where Adam went through?" Cynthia asked, handing him a bowl of soup as he came through the line.

"It's too much. Half the mountain came down there." Wyatt didn't soft-pedal the problem.

Connor spoke quickly. "We've been in communication with Adam, Cyn. He seems to be okay. He taps back promptly."

She nodded, accepting his words as they were meant— to comfort her and allay her fears. She saw Wyatt's glance go from her to Connor and back again, before he went on down the line. He and Connor had been the last to come in to eat.

"We're going to work shifts and dig all night," Connor told her, speaking low so as not to disturb others who had eaten and were now lying down. "Ranger and Harry will haul out the rock. We won't have to use the wheelbar-

row.'' He smiled at her, and she recalled her exhaustion
after only three trips.

''Poor beasts.''

''Get your dinner and come sit with me,'' he invited.

''I wanted to talk to Wyatt.''

''There's room. I think he saved you a place. Come on.''
He waited until she filled a bowl with steaming soup and
put a sandwich and some chips on a paper plate, then led
the way over to the bench where Wyatt was talking to Ted.

''There's another rainstorm due in tomorrow night,''
Ted told Connor and Cynthia when they were seated. ''I
was just asking Wyatt what he thought that might do.''

Cynthia looked up anxiously. Connor clasped her hand,
and she held his tightly while she waited for the expert as-
sessment.

''That could mean real trouble,'' Wyatt said, confirm-
ing her worst suspicions. ''The ground is already weak-
ened from water intrusion. There could be more slides.''
He smiled at Cynthia. ''I think we'll have your brother out
before then.''

''I hope so,'' she said fervently. She glanced down at her
and Connor's entwined hands. She let go and began to eat.
It wasn't until it was time to go to bed that she realized that
Ted MacCormick had brought cots for his men to use in
shifts and the families had brought camping gear. That left
Connor and her to find a place to sleep.

''You need to rest,'' she said, glancing over at him.
''There are two bunks in the cabin.''

For a second, their eyes met and exchanged a message
of other nights in another cabin, then Connor shook his
head. ''I'll be helping with Ranger and Harry tonight.
They're used to me. I'll sleep later.''

She nodded, refusing to let herself look at him again. After straightening up the makeshift kitchen, she lay down on her bed and tried to get some sleep.

Although her body trembled with fatigue, her mind wouldn't settle down. She thought of Adam, alone in the dark with no food and no blanket. At least the temperature would remain constant in the mine. The night air could drop to dangerously low levels in the mountains. She sighed tiredly and tried not to think. If she could only relax for a few minutes, she would sleep.

Her thoughts switched to Connor. She wasn't making the mistake of expecting anything from him—he had come out of human kindness—but she would always be grateful to him. Even though he obviously didn't want and wouldn't accept her gratitude, he had it anyway. He had earned it.

Some things were earned and some were given, she thought just before she went to sleep. Love was the finest gift of all.

Ten

In the early hours of the morning, when even the night creatures were still and dawn was only a hope in the heart, Connor silently entered the cabin. He closed the door and stood just inside the threshold.

The night chill had penetrated the walls, and he built up the dying fire in the fireplace. A smile hovered on his exhausted face as he lifted a lid from a pot on the stove and smelled the rich aroma of homemade soup. He swallowed a number of spoonfuls before replacing the lid.

Wearily he sat on the empty bunk and took his shoes off, all the time peering out the front windows. Outside were five tents in addition to the large one provided by the forestry service. The silence was so absolute, he felt as if he were inhabiting a ghost town. That was the way he had felt inside for a long time.

He rubbed a hand over his face as if he would erase the loneliness. The tightness in his chest warned him of his fatigue and his slipping control. He glanced across the room as Cynthia stirred in her sleep.

His eyes reflected the darkness, barely lit by the waning moon, as he looked at the silhouettes of the tents again. Each shelter contained friends of Cynthia; all had come to help her in her time of trouble.

Well, she had done enough for them. She deserved their help. He gazed with unconscious longing at her sleeping form, its gentle curves discernible under the cover. He had never met a person so full of love and concern for others, no matter what the expense to herself. But could she love only those who needed her? And when that need was gone, did her love go, too? A dismal ache swelled inside him.

The bond between brother and sister was strong and unwavering. She might have supported Adam, but Connor wouldn't classify the young man as incapacitated. Adam was as protective of Cyn as she was of him.

Connor wondered, what were her feelings for *him*? She had said she loved him, but that had been in passion. He didn't want her pity, but how he wanted her love...because he loved her.

He closed his eyes tightly. He had been drawn to her from the first moment he saw her standing in the sunlight with a smile on her lips and in her eyes.

How he loved her eyes—the way they crinkled at the corners when she laughed, the way they sparkled, the way they warmed him clear through when she looked at him.

Was the fierce, passionate attraction between them the start to winning her *true* love? She had been with no other, had chosen him as her lover. That had to indicate there was something special between them.

Still, she deserved someone better, he realized. A large knot formed in his chest at the thought of her with another. No, dammit, she was his. He would win her—but on his terms and in his own way.

Yes, he would have to make her see him as a man who could make it on his own. He wouldn't appeal to her sympathetic nature. She would have to come to him, loving him for himself, a man with his own strengths and faults, not some weakling to be shored up and guided in the right direction like a skid row derelict. Gritting his teeth, he stood and shucked his jeans, letting them fall in a heap on the floor.

When she moaned and thrashed around on her cot, he walked over to her and watched her, concerned. A small, sobbing sigh escaped her, and she turned restlessly. Without a moment's hesitation, he sat down on the narrow bed and gathered her into his arms.

"Connor?" she asked, her arm going around his neck.

"Yes. Go back to sleep. I've got you." He settled her on his lap, her face snuggled into his neck.

"Is there any news?"

"No."

"I'm scared," she admitted for the first time, her breathing uneven, her hands clutching him tightly.

"I know, Cyn," he said in a quiet tone. He didn't try to soothe away her fear, only to share it with her.

"Stay with me," she requested in a faint voice.

"I will." He curbed the elation that hearing she wanted him with her aroused. This was a time of trouble; emotions ran higher at these moments. He didn't let himself imagine it meant anything more. He must prove himself to her first. He had to earn her love.

Carefully, he laid her down and slid under the covers with her. Sighing, she rested against him, slipping her leg intimately between his. He smiled a bit. At this moment, he was so tired his body didn't even tense at her nearness.

Later, it did. He climbed out of her warm embrace and went to his cold bed sometime before dawn.

Cynthia woke, suddenly feeling cold and lonely. She saw Connor getting into Adam's bunk, having shed only his shoes and pants. He fell asleep as soon as his head touched his pillow.

She tried and failed to suppress the great tide of emotion that overwhelmed her when he was near. She longed to climb into his bed and back into his arms. That was where she belonged, whether he recognized it or not. Sighing, she scolded herself. This was not the moment for personal longing.

Glancing once more at him, she remembered the warmth of his arms around her. Or could it have been a dream? No, they had talked, then he had slept with her, letting her nestle against him.

She was unable to make herself believe he could share himself with her the way he had and not feel something more than desire. He had been thinking of her when he said they shouldn't see each other again after she told him she loved him. Did he merely like her, or feel a brotherly affection for her? No, their reactions toward each other were much too turbulent. It had to be more.

Shaking her head at her irrepressible optimism, she got up and dressed. She had other things to do.

She looked through Adam's pantry to see what she could add to breakfast in the main tent. She carried out all the eggs, some bread and tins of Canadian bacon. These were welcomed by the workers who were going back into the mine for a second turn. Those who had gotten off had, like Connor, wolfed down a sandwich and fallen into bed. Wyatt was asleep, too.

She and Trudy cooked the food and fed the men, then ate their own breakfast. She decided to go down and see how the new tunnel was progressing. It was disappointingly short.

"We've hit a solid rock wall," one of the rangers explained. "We're trying to go around it."

She went back to the surface and organized the families into teams again and sent them out to look for the old entrance, then paced restlessly until the helicopter flew in more supplies, which she made into fresh sandwiches and another pot of soup.

Connor came into the tent after a brief sleep. He looked strong and competent, but there were lines of fatigue on his face and a dark weariness in his eyes. She filled a plate for him.

"How's it going?" he asked while he ate.

Cynthia brought over a cup of coffee and sat on the bench opposite him. "Okay, I guess." She sighed and rubbed her fingers aimlessly over the surface of the table. "This waiting is terrible."

"Yes."

His glance was sympathetic. She thought she would collapse in his arms and cry on his shoulder if he acted kind. She got up and studied the maps. He came over and stood behind her.

"Are these the areas you've searched?" He reached around her and ran a finger over the marked zones.

"Yes. We've covered the whole mountainside."

"What about here?" He pointed to the ridge.

"That's too steep. It's a cliff that borders on the creek. There's too much loose stuff on the lower part and a sheer wall above."

Connor leaned over her shoulder while he studied the topographical map of the ridge. "The old prospectors tried to follow the gold up a creek until they found the mother lode. What if they found it and dug from the creek upward, following the trail of the deposit? A landslide could have closed it off years ago. Water running into the creek..." His voice trailed off. "You want to take a walk?"

"The ridge is dangerous along the creek," she warned.

His eyes darkened. "We'll be careful. Do you want to go or not?" He was determined to check the section out.

"I'll come."

They let Trudy know where they were going.

A few minutes later, Cynthia followed at Connor's heels. She marveled at his stamina as he walked briskly along a faint trail that was probably used by deer. Instead of staying on the ridge, he headed down the slope, choosing a route that would take them along a rocky protuberance a few feet above the rushing water.

After walking along a steep incline, she paused to catch her breath. Looking down, she saw an outcropping of rock that tripped a switch in her memory. "Connor, wait," she called to him, excitement in her voice.

He stopped and looked back. "Tired?" he asked, studying her gravely.

"No, no, it's the trail below." She pointed down the slope from them. "I remember playing with Adam there when we used to visit Uncle Abbott."

"So?"

"I'm sure there was a cave. Now it's gone. And there was a rock slide right in front of it. I remember because we had to be very careful climbing over the loose rocks to get to the cave. When Uncle Abbot found out where we were playing, he told us not to go there anymore."

Connor rubbed his chin. "Let's see if we can get down there. Do you remember where the cave was?"

"Yes, just a few feet over from those big boulders."

"Let's go."

They worked their way down to the boulders, then over onto some weed-covered rocks. The newer rock slide wasn't distinguishable from the old one that they used to climb over.

"It was right around here, I'm sure." She gauged their position from the seal rock and the creek. "I think...." Suddenly uncertain she glanced around her. Everything was different, and she no longer trusted her memory.

"Let's look around." Connor checked over the terrain, taking in the shape of the rock slide and the overhang of the ridge above them. "This is dangerous ground. The water undercuts the cliff here. That's why there have been so many slides. Be careful," he warned her unnecessarily.

They crawled over the rocks, poking under bushes and heavy growth for signs of the cave. They found nothing. Finally, Cynthia stood and arched her aching back. She surveyed the area. Something wasn't right.

"Connor, we're too far down," she called. "Look, the boulders have slipped down. That's what's wrong. The cave is higher."

They climbed up a number of feet, then renewed their search. Connor found the half-buried opening under a cover of wild blackberries.

"Ouch," he said. His shirt was caught on the bush across the back.

"Hold still." Cynthia worked the briars free from the material. Carefully, they cleared a path and peered into the dark passage. "Yes, this is it," she declared, sure now. She smiled radiantly at him.

He looked away from her, his manner remote. Her smile disappeared. "Let's go get Wyatt," he said.

"I'll start looking. You bring the others—"

"The hell you will," he snapped at her. "That's just what we need, two of you lost in there with a storm on the way. This area is primed for another slide."

"I won't get lost," she argued, determined to go ahead. "Adam and I played in here lots of times."

"Yeah, when you were kids visiting your uncle. How long ago was that?"

"Uncle Abbott died when I was thirteen." She gave him an angry glance, unable to admit he was right.

"Twelve years ago," Connor accurately assessed. "There's no way I'm going to let you traipse through those shafts. You don't know what has happened to them in all that time."

"Then let's both go. Adam might—"

"No," he told her in no uncertain terms.

"Yes," she said, just as stubborn.

He hauled her into his arms. "I'd go crazy," he muttered. Before letting her go, he kissed her until she was speechless. "Now, come on." He pushed her ahead of him, following her all the way back to the camp.

Wyatt was still asleep. When Connor woke him up and explained what they had found, Wyatt grabbed his shoes and put them on. "Lead the way." Ted MacCormick and two of his men accompanied them.

Cynthia fell into step behind the men. Connor glanced back, saw her and motioned for her to come to the front. "Lead on," he invited, surprising her. The men followed silently, and at last they reached the opening.

While the four experts considered the possibilities, Cynthia and Connor stood aside listening to the discussion. When she would have spoken up impatiently, he gripped her arm, warning her to be quiet. She gave him a dark look, which earned a frown from him.

She must have only dreamed he had been kind to her during the night, she decided. He obviously still felt the way he had when he had told her he didn't want to see her again.

"Cynthia has been in this mine. If we can get her inside, she might remember the direction the shaft runs. Let's try to clear these rocks and get a good look," Connor suggested, breaking into her distracted thoughts.

They talked it over and decided to go ahead. Carefully, they removed the rocky debris covering the entrance and stepped inside. Cynthia, looking around with the aid of their miner's lights, wondered if she really did recall the place. If she was right, there was one main passage and one smaller one.

Connor took her hand. "Ready?"

She went with him, guided by his flashlight. They came to a turnoff. "That doesn't go anywhere," she said. They walked on in the inky darkness, their footsteps muffled in the layers of dust that covered the floor.

They came to a rock wall. "Another cave-in," she said in despair. Tears sprang into her eyes and ran down her face.

"Buck up," Connor advised. "This is no time to cry."

Wyatt put an arm around her shoulders. His face was kind. "We'll dig through the other wall and find him," he promised.

"If it isn't too late," Connor said, reminding them that Adam's air supply might not last. He tapped on a rock, and the sound seemed loud in the gloomy air of the tunnel.

A tap came back to them from very close.

"Adam?" Cynthia called.

"Yeah, through here," he called back. "I'm in the old cave—"

"I *know* where you are now," she yelled, laughing and crying at the same time. She turned to Connor and threw her arms around him. "I knew you'd find him," she sobbed. "I knew you would."

He put her aside. "We have work to do," he said.

It took another four hours of digging to break through. Wyatt had the men shore up the walls of the old cavern around the slide area before he would allow removal of the talus to begin. Cynthia waited, by turns impatient and fearful. Each time a rock shifted, her heart gave a giant lurch.

Connor seemed to be everywhere. With his great strength and height, he hoisted support beams into place and held them while the other men nailed side posts on to brace them. He worked tirelessly until the job was done, then he stood aside as first Wyatt and then Cynthia went through the opening.

Adam lay on the floor in a pile of rubble. His left leg was trapped beneath the rocks. He grinned insouciantly at his rescuers and held up a small bag. "I've found it, Sis," he said, and passed out.

She rushed to him, took his face in her hands and stroked him lovingly.

"We'll have to move some of this stuff. It shouldn't take long." Wyatt called Connor and Ted in. There wasn't room for the other two men.

"You'll have to wait in the outer chamber," Connor told Cynthia. "We need the space to work."

"No, I want to stay with Adam." She sat in the dust with her brother's head in her lap.

"Get up, Cyn," Connor ordered her sternly.

"No." She glared defiantly at him. Didn't he understand that she couldn't leave Adam?

One hand on her arm and the other one under Adam's head brought her to her feet. "You're not doing him any good sitting there. Get out of here." Connor kept his voice low. After removing his shirt, he gently laid Adam's head on the flannel material. "There, he's fine." He sounded almost callous as he dismissed her.

"I hate you," she hissed, the sudden release of her fears shifting her emotions precariously.

They confronted each other. "Fine. Now that you've had your tantrum, get out of here." He turned back to the work at hand. She left the narrow space, and the other men cautiously entered the low chamber. She watched from the opening.

In another hour, they had Adam free. His broken leg was causing him a lot of pain, although he tried to smile when he came to.

"You've got a real lame duck to tend to this time," he said, spotting her just before the men lifted the beam that had fallen across his ankle. The easing of the pressure on his leg caused him to faint again.

One of the rangers strapped Adam's leg to a board, then they fastened him on a stretcher with a blanket around him and began the long trip back to the camp. Cynthia walked behind them anxiously as they negotiated the hazardous trail. Connor was last in line.

She glanced back once and saw him leaning against a tree. He looked exhausted, and she hesitated, wondering if she should go to him. When he saw her watching, he straightened and gave her a hard look before striding forward again. She would never understand him, she brooded as she walked on.

As they neared the clearing, she caught up with Wyatt, who was supporting the stretcher on one side of Adam's head. "I'll fly him out," she said.

Ted spoke up. "I sent for a helicopter with a medical crew aboard. It's already here."

Two women medics rushed forward and took over, checking Adam's vital signs and beginning an intravenous feeding to ward off shock. Cynthia stood helplessly aside as her brother was loaded onto the big chopper. When she started to climb on, too, she was told he would be taken to Lewiston.

"You can follow in your plane," Wyatt reminded her.

She could only watch as the helicopter lifted into the sky and veered off on a northwesterly course. She felt as if she were going to come apart as the helicopter disappeared from view. For two days, she'd kept her emotions tightly controlled. Now she scanned the clearing, filled with a need so great she couldn't deny it.

Her neighbors smiled at her, relieved that the rescue hadn't ended in tragedy. A smile brushed fleetingly over her trembly lips. When her eyes met a pair of jade-green ones, she felt as if the glance had penetrated clear to her soul.

For a long minute, they exchanged glances, and she saw in Connor a need, an inner agony, that could be comforted only in her arms, and she ached to hold him, to have his arms around her, to have him comfort her.

He turned away. She remembered him putting her aside earlier... just as he had his fiancée.

A ragged breath escaped her. She pressed her knuckles against her mouth, trying to hold in a sob. It was no use. She covered her face with her hands.

"There, there now. Go ahead and cry it out," a sympathetic voice murmured over her head. Wyatt pulled her against his chest and stroked her hair while she cried. When she looked up several minutes later, Connor was nowhere in sight.

"Would you like me to go to Lewiston with you?" Wyatt asked when she was calm. "I don't like the thought of you being alone." He handed her his handkerchief.

"You don't have to. I'll call my parents."

"I know I don't have to. I want to," Wyatt said, his gaze gentle as he watched her struggle with some inner problem.

"You're a good man," she quipped, forcing a lightness into her voice. "A real hero, always dashing to my rescue."

"Beautiful maidens are a specialty of mine." He grinned at her.

"Your teeth are straight," she remarked.

His smile widened. "Braces," he explained. "And I finally grew into my ears."

When he started laughing, she joined in, and the last of the tension disappeared. She left him and went to thank her neighbors for their help. After everyone had packed up and had started to head home, she paused and looked around the clearing. Ranger and Harry were gone, too. For a moment, she stared toward the woods, then she went to the cabin to clean up before she and Wyatt went to the hospital.

Feeling the weight in her pocket as she pulled off her jacket, she removed the bag Adam had handed her before he had passed out. She opened the drawstring and shook the contents into her palm. The bag was full of gold.

Eleven

Here," Wyatt said, handing Cynthia a cup of coffee.

"Thank you." She looked at him gratefully. "It's really wonderful of you to stay with me. As soon as my parents arrive, I'll fly you to Boise."

"You'll do no such thing," he informed her. "I'll take a commercial flight. You stay here. Adam will probably need you when he wakes up."

"If those nurses will let me in," she muttered, resentful at being excluded.

X rays had revealed that the damage to Adam's leg wasn't as extensive as they had first thought. He'd undergone surgery, and if there was no infection or other complication, the leg would eventually be as good as new.

Now Cynthia and Wyatt waited for Adam to come out of the recovery room. It seemed to be taking a long time. She worried that he was worse than they had told her; perhaps he had gone into severe shock.

A woman, tanned and shapely, her gray hair in a short, carefree style, entered the waiting room, followed by a man in his fifties, his handsome face lined with worry.

"Mom. Dad." Cynthia rushed across the room and hugged them both. "I'm so glad you're here."

"How is he?" her mother asked.

"He came through the surgery fine," Cynthia assured them. "Now we're waiting for him to come out of recovery." She turned to Wyatt. "This is Wyatt Carter. He lived in Portland—just down the street from us when we were children. He's the mining expert who came out with the rescue team. He saved Adam."

"Actually, I'm just the mining engineer who happened to be handy when they needed one," Wyatt said modestly, shaking hands with Alice Robards, then with Samuel. "Cynthia and Connor were the ones who found him."

"Adam was in a cave that was actually part of an old mine. We used to play in it when we visited Uncle Abbot. Look," she said, getting the bag of gold out of her purse. "Adam found this in there." She showed them the nuggets. "Remember the bag of gold found on Uncle Abbott? I think this came from the same cache."

While they waited to see Adam, they speculated on the gold and how it had come to be in the cave.

"I wonder if there's more," her father mused.

"We'll have to ask him when he comes to. I know that will be the first thought in his mind," Cynthia predicted.

It wasn't until they were told that Adam was being taken to his room that Wyatt stood to leave. "Everything seems to be under control, so I'll get back to work. It was nice meeting you," he said cordially to her parents before turning to her. "I'll be in Boise off and on for the next few months. May I call you?"

Cynthia walked him to the door. "Of course. I love hearing from old friends." She gave him a warm smile.

"I was madly in love with you years ago. Do you remember?" he asked, a reminiscent light in his eyes, along with a spark of interest that went deeper than childhood memories.

"That was a long time ago," she said with no encouragement in her voice.

He looked mildly disappointed at her lack of response. "Well, I'll be on my way."

"Goodbye, and thanks for all your help. Everyone was wonderful." She stayed at the door until his cab pulled out of sight. Her mind wasn't on her childhood friend, though. All her thoughts were on the unfathomable male she had met in June and hadn't been able to forget. She had to know exactly where she stood with Connor. And she meant to find out . . . soon.

"We can go to Adam now," her father said upon her return. "He's awake." They followed a nurse along the hallway.

To Adam's and Cynthia's amazement, their mother began weeping when she entered the room and saw his pale but bravely smiling face. She hugged Adam, careful of his leg, which was in traction, with a cast on his foot and lower leg.

Adam patted her awkwardly, flushing as tears came to his own eyes. Finally, Mr. Robards lifted his wife from the bed. "There now, Alice, you'll dissolve the cast if you keep that up, and they'll have to take him back to the operating room."

Mrs. Robards laughed shakily and blew her nose on her husband's handkerchief. "I'm sorry for going soggy on you. I was just so worried when Cynthia called and said you had been hurt. It . . . it just got to me all at once.''

"You're looking pretty good after your ordeal," Mr. Robards commented, shaking hands with his son. He further surprised his children by bending down and kissing Adam on the forehead.

Adam looked at his sister as if to ask, "What gives?"

She grinned and wrinkled her nose at him. It seemed her parents had forgiven their black sheep for his shortcomings.

On an impulse, she left the other three alone to talk and discover one another. Perhaps it was a turning point in their relationship.

Going to a window, she gazed out at the sky. It was late, and the threatening storm had blown in, bringing the rain that she had so dreaded while Adam was still trapped in the mine. There would probably be more cave-ins. She was going to have to dissuade Adam from going back. It wouldn't be easy; it would probably be as hard as convincing her never to return to Connor O'Shaugnessy.

Unwittingly, she blinked back tears and wondered if it would always be like this, if thoughts of Connor would intrude when her defenses were low, as they were now. She longed for the comfort of his arms. No one else would do. Wyatt was nice, but he wasn't the one her heart yearned for. Only Connor filled her spirit with love.

She remembered the sound of the raindrops against the windows of the cabin, whispering of enchantment while she and Connor had made love. She remembered his eyes and how beautiful they were in the sunlight . . . or shining in the firelight.

In that moment before he had turned from her in the clearing, she was sure she had seen a reflection of her own pain and longing in those verdant depths, and then he had left without saying goodbye.

Tears shimmered in her eyes, turning them to liquid gold. She breathed deeply for several minutes. When her father came to her, she was calm once more. She went in to see Adam.

"Did you go back into the cave?" he demanded the next afternoon when he and Cynthia were alone for the first time.

"Don't be a dope. All I wanted to do was get you out."

He lowered his voice. "Did I give you anything?" he asked.

She reached nonchalantly into her purse. "Like this old tobacco pouch?"

He grabbed it from her, wincing as he stretched sore muscles. "Yeah. There's more where this came from."

"You're not going back in those mines," she said in alarm.

"Yes, I am. But only to get the other four bags just like this one. There're two old miners in there, Cyn."

She flinched as he used Connor's nickname for her. "Two miners?"

"Their skeletons. I think somebody killed them and stashed the bodies there, intending to come back for the gold later—there would have been six bags—but didn't make it for some reason."

"Maybe a slide hid the opening."

"It was easy to find when we were kids."

"Maybe a later one opened it up again." She waved the discussion aside. "That doesn't matter. Adam, I'm serious. It's too dangerous for you to dig in those old tunnels."

"I'm not going to. I just want those other bags so I can pay my way through school. I can't live off you forever."

"School?" she repeated. "What school?"

"Archaeology," he said smugly. "That's what I want to study. When I found those two old skeletons, it was like a light came on in my brain. I've always loved digging around and finding things, arrowheads and such, when we were little, remember?"

"Yes." Her eyes began to take on the sparkle of his. "Oh, yes, love, that would be perfect for you." She leaped up from her chair and threw her arms around his neck. "You can live with me and go to school in Boise."

He patted her back. "Sorry, but I'm going to the University of California. A friend was telling me about a program they have there...."

For the rest of the afternoon they discussed his plans.

"Dad said he would pay my way, but I'd rather do it on my own. The only thing that bothers me," he mentioned later, "is the fact that you took that mail job on my account. Now you'll be stuck with it."

"That doesn't matter. My contract is up in March. That's only a few months from now. Maybe I'll do something else."

"What?"

"I don't know."

"Go to school with me," Adam suggested. "You can get your master's degree. Or change to archaeology."

She laughed. "Old bones don't turn me on the way they do you," she teased. "I'll stay put."

"Okay," he said, then abruptly changed the subject. "Say, did you notice there's something different about the folks?"

"Yes. They really were shook up when you got hurt. I think they love you. I can't imagine why."

She dodged his feeble attempt at a blow and left him happily making plans to retrieve his treasure. Leaving him in the capable hands of her parents and the doctors, she climbed into her plane and flew to Boise to pick up the mail. Mixed in with her official chores was one more task....

On Friday of the week following the rescue, she was finally caught up on her postal route and able to drop into Connor's place. It was after three when she arrived. She had skipped lunch and was free for the rest of the weekend, a part of the plot she had planned very carefully. If the confrontation worked as she hoped, she would be staying.

Her nerves tingled as she tied up and approached the house. She knew now that she hadn't been mistaken about the look in his eyes when he left Adam's place. She was going to ask him straight out what he was going to do about their relationship. That should give him something to think about. Tilting her chin at a defiant angle, she marched up to the front door and went in without knocking.

There was no one inside. The fireplace was cleaned out, and the furniture was covered with sheets. An air of desolation hung over the cabin. She ran down to the mailbox and looked inside. A note for her was waiting:

Cyn,
I've taken a job with Graceson Construction on a road to be cut through to the Big Creek project. Would you hold my mail for me until I know what my address will be?'

Connor

It took a minute for the impact of his message to sink in. He was gone. Just like that. Her gaze wandered over the sun-glazed meadow and upward to the far mountains, but she saw only darkness. The sun's warmth was lost on her shivering limbs. It was as if a wilderness had suddenly engulfed her heart.

Sitting down on the wharf, her mind in a haze, she ate her lunch, her only company the bees droning busily over the flowers. The waters of the nearby creek rushed toward the river like an impatient lover eager to join his mate.

August passed into September. Cynthia finished her mail run early on the third Friday of the month and returned to her apartment. She had no special plans. She thought of flying to visit with her parents but couldn't muster any enthusiasm for the trip.

The telephone started to ring when she let herself in. She dashed to answer it. ''Hello.''

''Cyn, this is Connor.''

The memory of a day in June flashed into her mind ... the way he had looked, standing there in the radiant light, his hair like dark flames around his head, his body a living memorial to excellence in the human form. The way she had wanted to touch him ...

''Are you there?''

''Yes. Yes, I am,'' she said, stumbling over the words. ''How nice to hear from you.'' Brilliant opening line, she chided herself. She sounded just like her Great-Aunt Martha—formal and prudish.

''Look, I'm calling to ask if you'd like to visit the project I'm working on. It would be a weekend trip. We could drive up tomorrow, explore the area, get in some fishing and come back Sunday. . . . If you're free,'' he tacked on.

She thought of a thousand reasons why she shouldn't go, and only one for going. She wanted to see him. "Yes, I can go." Was that her voice, so cool and controlled?

"Fine. I'll see you about eight. It's a long trip, so we'll need an early start."

"I'll be ready." She hung up when he said goodbye. For a long minute, she stayed by the phone, wondering why he had invited her. He had sounded polite but remote. Shaking her head at the vagaries of life, she went to find her overnight bag.

Cynthia rushed to the window as soon as she woke the next morning. The day was clear and warm. She quickly showered and dressed and finished packing. To prove to herself that she had no high expectations, she ignored her lacy nightgowns in favor of her usual nightshirt, which hung to her knees.

Connor arrived promptly at eight. He looked wonderful in a comfortable-looking pair of faded cords and a red pullover shirt. He looked her over in a cool appraisal.

"Beautiful as ever," he murmured, taking her bag.

"Thank you." She refrained from telling him that he was the only one who saw her that way. "Where exactly are we going?" she asked instead. He escorted her to the street.

"Up past Arrowrock Reservoir, along the middle fork of the Boise River, then over a dirt road northeast toward Galena Peak," he answered precisely. "It's less than a hundred miles as the crow flies, but it'll take us about four hours to get there. I've brought lunch to eat on the way."

"Is this yours?" She asked as she climbed into the four-wheel-drive vehicle.

"Yeah. Brand-new. How do you like it?" He started the engine and pulled into the traffic.

"It's nice, very plush. I like being higher than the other cars. Gives me a feeling of superiority," she replied.

He laughed as she looked down her nose at the autos on the busy road. "Find us some music," he suggested.

She turned the dial to her favorite station of light rock, and they sang along to the tunes they knew. The morning passed swiftly. They stopped a little after eleven and ate by the roadside, then he pushed on, explaining he wanted to see the foreman before the men knocked off for the day.

"I see." So there would be other people present. This was only a trip to show her how well he was doing, she decided. Fine. Now she could stop wondering about his intentions.

An hour later, they drove into a clearing beside a huge earthwork. "The roadbed," he said, pointing at the site.

She saw the site for the new road. The earthwork rose steeply from the flatter ground, and a bridge would span the distance from one rise to the next, which was in the process of being built across the narrow canyon.

"What a huge prospect!" she exclaimed, in awe of the formidable task.

"This is a five-year job. I'll have to be moving around a lot for the next few years." He hesitated. "It will be a rough life," he added truthfully.

"Yes, but it could be fun, too."

"You think so?"

Their eyes met, and something in his gaze made her heart beat faster.

"You don't think it would be too hard a life on a woman or a family to be on the move for that long? I'll be going to the main headquarters in Seattle eventually."

"Where would your family live?" she asked. Pain constricted her throat; her voice was husky. Was he thinking of pursuing his fiancée again?

"Come on. I'll show you."

He led the way to a trailer set back among the trees at one side of the clearing. Another, much larger trailer was the office. Others housed the work crew.

He held the door open, allowing her to enter first. The trailer was simple and clean; the kitchen was in the middle, the living room to the right and the bedroom and bath to the left.

He explained his plans. "I was thinking of buying a place in Boise, in order to have a permanent base—a place to stay on weekends."

"That sounds like a good idea." His wife and kids could stay in town while he was out on the job, she supposed. The idea angered her. In fact, she was getting darned mad, period. Why had she let herself in for this torture? She must have been crazy to come here. Had she thought he would take one look and confess his undying love for her?

"You can sleep in here. I'll take the couch." He put her overnight bag next to the bed.

"You'd better keep the bed. You'll hang off both ends of the sofa," she said lightly, eyeing his length.

"No. I want you in the bedroom. You can close and lock the door tonight." He chucked her under the chin, then ruffled her curls, laughing as if it were a big joke. She refrained from telling him to mind his own virtue, if that was what the locked door was all about.

He certainly seemed in rare spirits, she observed later as she followed him around the camp. While he consulted with his foreman, she looked over the drawings and maps. The new road would replace an old one, eliminating many of the dangerous curves and slopes.

She knew she had no right to, but she was proud of Connor's part in the project and of the respect the burly foreman evidently had for him. She was sure he had had to work hard to prove himself to the tough construction crew during the past weeks. From the greetings he received when they left the office and climbed the rocks to the roadbed, it was plain that he had succeeded.

"Hey, look what the boss brought back from his trip into town," one of the rowdier ones called out as the men took a break. "No wonder he was up at the crack of dawn, cleaning everything, before he spruced himself up and took off."

Cynthia was amazed as Connor's ears turned red. At his rueful glance, she grinned broadly at him. "You did a good job," she said.

"Thanks."

He introduced her to a couple of the men, stating her name with no further explanation of her presence. She knew there was a lot of speculation among them, but they kept quiet within Connor's protective proximity.

That night the men dispersed either to the other trailers or to the nearest town, where their families or girlfriends waited. She and Connor went to his place, where he cooked steaks on a portable grill while she watched the French fries in the kitchen. They had wine and salad with the meal.

After dinner, they listened to records, and he told her all about his job. "So that's the general scope of it," he concluded three hours later. "I don't think I've ever talked so much at one time in my life. You're a good listener."

"It was interesting," she told him sincerely.

"How do you think a woman would feel about living here?"

"I can't speak for all women," she began slowly, "but I would certainly want to be with my husband, wherever he was. If we had school-age children, it would be a different matter. We would have to consider them."

"That's what I thought, too."

He fell into an introspective mood after that, and they didn't talk much. Cynthia felt resentful, being used to sound out his misgivings about a woman at the site. Unless she were the woman he had in mind, of course. She had to smile at her own foolishness.

Connor glanced at her and saw the smile. Rising, he yawned, and his shirt stretched across his broad chest, making her want to slip her fingers inside and comb through the thick, wiry curls. She looked away. He was too dangerous to her peace of mind.

He came to her and sat on the arm of her chair. He fastened his gaze on her mouth, and she heard him draw a deep breath and let it out slowly. She recalled the movement of his chest against hers when they had made love...the quick intake of breath, the sudden release.

"I thought I could stay away from you, but I can't," he said. He stroked her arm from wrist to elbow.

When she looked up, his lips covered hers and his tongue invaded the silken depths of her mouth. The kiss was sudden, fiery and dazzling, shaking her with its passion.

She gave herself up to the embrace. She had missed him more than she had realized. Her heart insisted that this was the right place for her. She desperately wanted to believe it. She wanted him to see it, too. There was no better time to prove it to him than now, she decided with love's independent logic. As the kiss deepened, she forgot reasoning and found only pleasure.

He moved his hands over her and opened her shirt to caress her breasts. He made a low growl in his throat, and she answered with a sigh of happiness.

"Connor," she whispered, wanting more from him.

Her voice seemed to break the spell. He wrenched himself away from her and paced several steps across the room. He seemed to be angry with himself. "I'm sorry, Cyn. I never meant that to happen. I didn't bring you here to satisfy my lust."

"That's okay." Her voice was a little shaky as she brought her confused emotions back under control.

"No, dammit, it's not all right." He strode across the narrow room and back. "I apologize. It won't happen again," he promised. He ran a hand over his face wearily. "Go to bed now. Please. And lock your door."

Giving her a pained smile, he walked out into the cold night, leaving her to wonder just what was going on. Taking his advice, she prepared for bed and climbed in between the sheets. The mattress felt hard and strange to her. She wished she were safe at home in her own bed.

She woke at six on Sunday morning. The sky was cloudy and a mist hung over the valley, low and wispy, but she thought it would clear up as the sun warmed the air.

She showered and dressed quickly. When she went into the kitchen, Connor was already there, cooking sausages. At her appearance, he put bread in the toaster and fried some eggs. She poured the coffee and buttered the toast when it popped up.

"Good morning," he said solemnly when they were seated at the table.

"Good morning." She smiled at him.

During the night, she had arrived at the undeniable conclusion that Connor wanted her. That much had been obvious from their kiss. He also had a certain amount of regard for her, which complicated the issue.

He had never wanted to get involved with her, and she had to respect his wishes. She couldn't demand that he love her. Life didn't work that way. There was only one thing to do, only one solution that would work.

"You're quiet this morning," he commented.

She tilted her head. "You prefer chatter?"

"I think I'd prefer anything but silence." His smile was endearing. "Are you angry about last night?"

"No." That was the truth.

"Cyn," he said seriously. "I'd like for us to be friends. I know there have been a lot of problems in our relationship, but let's start over as of today. Could we?"

Now was the time, but she couldn't get the words past her throat. One day of fun—that was all she wanted. She nodded.

Connor felt only minor relief. He still had a long way to go before she looked at him the way she had looked at Wyatt. He wanted to win her respect and friendship before he began his courtship. That was the only way he could be sure she wanted him for himself and not as part of some sympathetic response to his past problems.

He took her fishing at his favorite place that morning. They caught five trout, three of them on her line and two on his. They cooked the fish for lunch before he drove her back to Boise in the early afternoon. They had talked of trivialities all day, carefully avoiding anything personal.

"Would you like to have dinner with me?" he invited as she dug out the key to her apartment. "I know a spaghetti—"

"I think not. I'm tired, and I have a busy day tomorrow. Would you like some coffee?" So polite, she thought. She had to tell him now.

"I think I'd better get back," he said, his voice suddenly husky. "The roads can get treacherous after dark.

Listen, I think I can get to town next weekend. Let's go to a movie."

She shook her head. "I've promised next weekend to my parents." She paused. "I don't think it's a good idea for us to see each other again." There, she'd finally gotten the words out.

She met his gaze levelly. He looked exactly as he had the first time she saw him—angry and frustrated. Her own anger stirred. Did he think she was at his beck and call? She had her own life to live, and it was best to get on with it.

"I don't want to see you again, Connor."

"Why not?" he demanded.

"I just don't see any need. You have your life, and I have mine."

"And never the twain shall meet?" he challenged her.

"Yes."

"Have I proven myself to you?" he asked. "Now that I no longer need your interference and guidance, you're telling me goodbye. Is that how you see it?"

"It isn't that at all," she said heatedly.

"That's the way I see it." He ignored her protest. "How about one for the road, then?"

Before she could respond, he hauled her into his arms, settling his lips over hers with unerring accuracy. He kissed her until she was hopelessly lost in the bliss, wanting him more than anything in life. She put her arms around him and kissed him with as much force, as much passion, as he did her. When they at last drew apart, he stared at her for a long minute.

"How do you always manage to turn the tables on me?" he asked, an ironic smile lifting one corner of his mouth.

He released her and stepped away. "I'm not through with you yet."

"I'm through with you," she informed his rapidly receding back. She went in and slammed the door, angrier than she could ever remember. From this minute, she was going to forget she had ever known Connor O'Shaugnessy.

He realized he might never see her again until next spring,
if ever.

"It's too much—" A voice in the darkness interrupted the
evening hush. She was closer now, coming up the road, holding
her son in her arms. "I can't do it." From his own fire, Connor
smiled. In a few minutes she had found the fire.

Twelve

—

On the following Friday, Cynthia made her rounds on
both sides of the river and finished by two o'clock. Several of the families were having a get-together before winter set in, but she had declined their invitation to join them
for the weekend. Instead, she flew back to Boise, choosing a course that would take her over Connor's cabin.
Maybe she would stay there, she thought, feeling somewhat melancholy. Heavy clouds promised rain before
nightfall.

Several Day-Glo flags caught her eye, and she dropped
lower to investigate. A red bandanna fluttered from the
mailbox. Connor appeared to be in residence.

She flew over the lagoon, banked and turned back. She
didn't want to see him, but technically, she was supposed
to stop. Circling again, she set the plane lightly down on
the calm surface of the water.

After tying up, she opened the crudely built mailbox and found a note for her inside. It told her to follow the red string. She looked around. Sure enough, there was a thin red cord tied to the pier. It led her up the path to the front porch of Connor's house.

The door opened before she could knock. He looked her over hungrily.

"Hello, Cyn," Connor said. "Come in. Lunch is ready."

She stepped over the threshold warily. She wasn't sure she could stand being so close to him.

He grinned. "Don't be afraid."

"I'm not."

"Come into the kitchen," he invited her.

Angling her chin determinedly, she followed his directions. The table was set for two. A vase of dried grasses decorated the center of the blue tablecloth.

"Beef stew," he told her, spooning up big bowls for them. He finished preparing the meal while she stood by her usual chair. When he pulled it out, she sat down. He leaned over her, and for a second, she thought he was going to kiss her, but he didn't. He went to his chair, and she breathed again.

He looked wonderful in a plaid wool shirt and navy cords. He filled out his clothing in a very attractive, masculine way. She swallowed the first spoonful with difficulty.

After a few minutes of silence, she said, "This is a real treat. Your stew is unbeatable." She wondered if her smile was as tremulous as her stomach.

"Barney gave me this recipe."

Pleasure radiated from his face. He looked happy in a way she had never seen him before. She wanted to ask him a million questions, but she settled on one for a start. "What are you doing here?"

"Just relaxing for a couple of days."

"I see. Oh, I saw the article in the paper on your road project. It quoted Mr. Graceson as being very pleased with your talent and said you had been put in charge of all the bridges. Congratulations."

"Graceson is a good man to work for," Connor murmured.

She glanced at him but had to look away quickly. His eyes were darkly disturbing, burning with mysterious flames that seemed to sear right down to the very center of her. Why was he staring at her like that?

"How's your family?" he asked.

"Fine." She recounted Adam's latest plan. "I think archaeology is just the field for him," she concluded.

"I can tell you're pleased." His smile played over her like sunbeams warming a flowery meadow. "Did you lecture him about going back into the mine?"

A flush crept into her cheeks. "A little, but he had to have his other bags of gold, so I flew him in and out in the same day after he got out of the hospital."

"That's like you." His tone was so tender she thought she would give in to it and had to remind herself of her firm decision to stay away from him.

Since the weekend at his trailer, she'd realized that he didn't love her at all and had come to terms with reality. She was glad he was doing well, that he liked his boss and his boss liked him. And she was relieved to find herself firmly in control of her emotions.

They ate in silence for a while. She looked up and met his gaze—the hunger was unmistakable. She recognized it because it matched the hunger building in her. She shouldn't have come inside for lunch. They couldn't evade their passion; it was as inevitable as the sun rising over the Bitterroot mountains.

"What?" he asked, studying her closely. A smile lurked around the corners of his mouth, and she realized she had been thinking aloud.

"Nothing. I was just thinking."

"What about?"

"It wasn't important."

"I'm not going to give up until you tell me."

Her face flushed with anger. "I said it didn't matter," she said, her voice rising.

"Do you want to watch the sunrise with me?" The question was an invitation.

"No," she snapped.

His laughter surprised her. "I'd like to watch it with you. I'd like to do a lot of things with you. Eat all our meals together. Watch each new day come in. Make love with you."

She stared at him.

"Finish your meal. We'll talk later," he said.

Leaving her with a thousand questions, he calmly went on eating. She polished off the remainder of the stew and homemade bread, then gulped her milk down. He finished when she did.

"Let's take our coffee into the living room," he suggested.

She followed him and sat on the sofa while he added logs to the fire until it crackled merrily.

"Now." He placed his cup on the end table and removed hers from her grip. He sat down beside her and took her hands in his. He caressed each of her fingers before he brought them to his mouth and kissed them.

Cynthia watched, fascinated. Was this the beginning of a seduction in front of the fire? The bearskin rug was in place....

"I'm not going to have an affair with you," she stated firmly.

"Why not?" He leaned over her and nuzzled her throat, his touch playing havoc with her resolve.

"It isn't right."

"Yes, it is." He lifted his head and gazed into her defiant eyes. "I was wrong before, Cyn. You knew all along what was right for me."

"Thank you," she said coolly, masking the hot flames of desire that seared her heart.

"Do you still love me?"

The question left her speechless. She remembered how she had felt when he had turned away from her and left Adam's place without saying goodbye, and all her resentment returned. "I never want to see you again as long as I live," she declared, pushing against his chest.

He threw back his head and laughed as if that were the most wonderful news he had ever heard. "Then you don't feel that you have to keep on seeing me just because you feel sorry for me?"

"Of course not." She was exasperated with him. "I haven't felt the least bit sorry for you since the moment I saw you standing in the sun chopping wood, determined to hate the world."

"Good." He took a deep breath. "I love you," he murmured softly.

"You don't," she denied.

"I love you," he repeated firmly. "And you love me."

"You thought I was trying to take over and run your life. You didn't believe in my love."

"I was wrong, but there were extenuating circumstances. The trial and the other engagement—all that blinded me to the real thing." His mouth moved toward hers.

"You can't change your mind like that."

He sighed heavily. "Are you going to lecture me about it? Why can't I love you? I've wanted you since the first minute I saw you. Since then, my need for you has only grown stronger with each passing day."

"You've only seen me once in over a month. You didn't say one word to me after the rescue, just got on Ranger and rode off. Why didn't you tell me this when you took me to see your road construction project?" With a certain amount of irony, she realized she was arguing against their involvement when only a few weeks before she had come here determined to force him to admit his feelings.

"I had to prove to you I could make it on my own without you running interference for me. I can find my own jobs, Cyn. The one thing I can't do is live without you."

He met her eyes without making any move to touch her again. A long minute passed, then another. Tentatively, she reached out to him and stroked the lock of hair that fell over his forehead. He closed his eyes and sighed. Then he gathered her into his arms, his lips seeking hers.

She met his kiss, hesitantly at first, then eagerly, as he held her closer, taking her love and returning it with his. She felt the tremor that raced through his strong frame and held on to him as tightly as she could.

He explored her mouth thoroughly, finding all the sweetness that she possessed. Their tongues engaged in the serious play of passion, and she responded to every demand he made. When they could hardly breathe, he lifted his head and smiled down at her.

"I love you," he said. "I don't think I can tell you how much. I'll never walk away from you again. That day, when Adam was safe, and you looked at me...you'll never know how much I needed to come to you then, to hold you and comfort you. But I couldn't, Cyn. I needed to come to you in strength, as a whole man. Do you understand?"

"Yes," she whispered. The love she had tried to deny expanded in her slender body until it was too much for her to bear. "Make love to me," she pleaded. "I need you."

Connor reveled in her love. It poured over him like healing balm, and he felt proud and worthy of her, his own love for her strong and sure and endless.

"I love you. Cyn, I love you."

He quickly prepared a bed for them with the comforter spread over the rug. When he had her undressed, he laid her there. Her golden eyes watched as he stripped out of his clothing.

Her smile was full of love as she snuggled into his embrace. She sighed as his body settled lightly over hers, covering her with the magic fire of his touch. She felt reborn like the phoenix that rose from the flames of its own ashes. The fire of their love made her feel whole again.

With increasing urgency, he melded them into one, bringing from her a cry of happiness. His eyes never left hers as he applied all the skill and knowledge he had gained in loving her to making this time the best ever for her. When her cry became one of fulfillment, he sought his release.

For a long time, they rested together, sleeping or just watching the flames dancing in the fireplace. After a while, he kissed her and began to love her all over again.

"Adam found his treasure in the mine," he murmured, "and I found mine in you."

Outside, the rain began to fall, and the water rushed with mindless energy to join the creek, the river, the sea. Inside the cabin, there was only the crackle of the fire . . . and the sweet sharing of golden dreams.

* * * * *

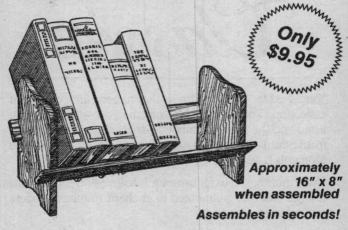

Silhouette Romance™
Legendary Lovers Trilogy

BY DEBBIE MACOMBER....

ONCE UPON A TIME, in a land not so far away, there lived a girl, Debbie Macomber, who grew up dreaming of castles, white knights and princes on fiery steeds. Her family was an ordinary one with a mother and father and one wicked brother, who sold copies of her diary to all the boys in her junior high class.

One day, when Debbie was only nineteen, a handsome electrician drove by in a shiny black convertible. Now Debbie knew a prince when she saw one, and before long they lived in a two-bedroom cottage surrounded by a white picket fence.

As often happens when a damsel fair meets her prince charming, children followed, and soon the two-bedroom cottage became a four-bedroom castle. The kingdom flourished and prospered, and between soccer games and car pools, ballet classes and clarinet lessons, Debbie thought about love and enchantment and the magic of romance.

One day Debbie said, "What this country needs is a good fairy tale." She remembered how well her diary had sold and she dreamed again of castles, white knights and princes on fiery steeds. And so the stories of Cinderella, Beauty and the Beast, and Snow White were reborn....

Look for Debbie Macomber's *Legendary Lovers* trilogy from Silhouette Romance: *Cindy and the Prince* (January, 1988); *Some Kind of Wonderful* (March, 1988); *Almost Paradise* (May, 1988). Don't miss them!

SRT-1

Silhouette Intimate Moments

NEXT MONTH
CHECK IN TO
DODD MEMORIAL HOSPITAL!

Not feeling sick, you say? That's all right, because Dodd Memorial isn't your average hospital. At Dodd Memorial you don't need to be a patient—or even a doctor yourself!—to examine the private lives of the doctors and nurses who spend as much time healing broken hearts as they do healing broken bones.

In UNDER SUSPICION (Intimate Moments #229) intern Allison Schuyler and Chief Resident Cruz Gallego strike sparks from the moment they meet, but they end up with a lot more than love on their minds when someone starts stealing drugs—and Allison becomes the main suspect.

In May look for AFTER MIDNIGHT (Intimate Moments #237) and finish the trilogy in July with HEARTBEATS (Intimate Moments #245).

Author Lucy Hamilton is a former medical librarian whose husband is a doctor. Let her check you in to Dodd Memorial—you won't want to check out!

IM229-1